Chance
Awakening

Chance Awakening

George Markstein

BALLANTINE BOOKS • NEW YORK

Some of the fiction in this story
is fact. Some of the fact is fiction.
GM

This edition published by arrangement with
Souvenir Press Ltd.

Manufactured in the United States of America

First Ballantine Books Hardcover Edition: September 1978

Library of Congress Cataloging in Publication Data

Markstein, George.
    Chance awakening.

    I. title.
PZ4.M3478Ch 1978 [PR6063.A644] 823′.9′14 78-17501
ISBN 0-345-27717-1

For J, always.
Only she knows
the code.

Shake off this downy sleep, death's counterfeit,
And look on death itself.

Macbeth
Act II

London

1

The man screamed as he fell out of the fifth-floor window, but nobody heard him above the noise of the traffic in nearby Piccadilly. He plunged down into Dover Street, narrowly missing the bronze statue of the naked horse-rider, and it wasn't until he crashed on the pavement that he was noticed.

A couple of people stared, disbelieving, at the broken figure sprawled near a parked car. A woman stifled her panic with a fist in her mouth. A man with long hair ran forward to take a closer look at the body.

Across the street, Baron automatically looked up at the fifth floor. The window was open. That was all, of course. No face. Nobody peering out.

As he ran across the road, Baron wondered what exactly he should do. He was on surveillance duty, following Hentoff. Hentoff had gone into the building, and Baron had been waiting patiently for him to come out.

A small crowd began to gather. Baron pushed his way through, muttering politely, "Excuse me." He could have been very official about it, and taken charge, but that wasn't his job here.

Although the man was dead, there was surprisingly little blood. His legs were at a curious, twisted angle.

Baron knew it instinctively before he even saw the face. The man was Hentoff.

He had seen many photographs of Hentoff, some blurred, some quite sharp, all taken surreptitiously while they were tailing the man. Baron had one in his pocket. It had been issued to all of them.

But, in shadowing him, Baron had always had to keep a discreet distance, sometimes on the other side of the street, sometimes thirty or forty yards behind. Only now, in death, did he get his first close-up look at the face of the man who was on the department's No. 1 list.

"Stand back, everybody," said a voice. A policeman appeared. Baron decided he had better stay anonymous. The helmets were taking over. There'd be publicity. An inquest. He didn't want his name taken. And he had to keep the department out of it.

"Did you see it?" asked the policeman.

Baron shook his head.

"Anybody see him fall?"

Heads craned upwards. The tell-tale window on the fifth floor was still open.

In the distance, sirens. Somebody must have dialed 999. Baron melted just as the first police car appeared, blue light flashing.

Baron called the office from Green Park Station.

"What do you mean, he *fell?*"

Foxglove was in an irritable mood.

"Fell, jumped, was pushed, I don't know," said Baron. It was hot in the phone booth. "Anyway, he's dead."

"People don't just *fall.*"

Baron cut it short. "What do you want me to do?"

There was a pause. Then: "Nothing more you can do, is there?" It sounded rather reproachful. "Better come in and do your report. We'll keep Special Branch posted."

"All right," said Baron.

"You're sure you didn't see anybody with him just before it happened?"

"No," said Baron.

"Pity."

Outside the station, an ambulance went screaming past the Ritz. *Au revoir,* Hentoff, thought Baron.

4

He decided to walk back to the office. He could save the cab fare, and then claim it on expenses.

He strolled across Berkeley Square and wondered how to write a report about the death of Hentoff, travel agent, gambler, man-about-town.

And the best operator Soviet intelligence had in London.

It had to be a good report. Baron didn't want any trouble.

2

Michael Golly walked over to the massed rows of tanks and armored cars, and inspected them.

He picked up a small model of a Ferret scout car, and examined it.

"Can I help you?" asked the sales girl. She was pretty, and she liked working in a toyshop. It was more fun than her last job—trying shoes on sweaty feet.

"I'm just looking," said Golly, and put down the Ferret.

"Any little boy would like one of these," said the girl, encouragingly.

"It's not for a little boy," said Golly.

He glanced over the ranks of models. "Has anything new come in?"

Some men will never grow up, thought the girl. But she wasn't laughing at him. She rather liked him. She thought she wouldn't mind if he tried to chat her up.

"This is a nice one," she said, and held up a Chieftain tank. Temptingly, she turned the turret.

Golly shook his head. "Sorry," he said. "That's been around a long time."

"You collect them?"

He smiled at her.

"I make them."

Golly liked to visit toyshops, and see if there was anything new in the way of military models. Although he knew the market well, and kept up to date on new production lines, there might always be a surprise. A new French model. Or something the Germans had thought up.

And Golly didn't like such surprises. He preferred to know about things as early as possible.

"Ah, well," said the girl, a little sadly. "I don't suppose I have anything you want."

"There's always next time," said Golly.

I really would like to have sold him something, she thought, as she watched him walk away.

Golly came out of the toyshop into Regent Street, and bought an evening paper. The item in the stop-press column about a travel agent called Hentoff falling to his death from an office building in Dover Street meant nothing to him.

Not then.

3

They were not pleased with Baron. He knew that as soon as Foxglove asked to see him.

The Hentoff file was on the desk in front of him.

"Didn't you wonder what he was doing in the building?" asked Foxglove.

"I thought we could check on that later," said Baron. "The thing was to keep tabs on him when he came out."

Foxglove sniffed. "So you just stood there? Didn't go into the building after him or anything?"

"I followed the routine. I waited for him outside. What was I supposed to do, go up in the same lift with him?"

Baron felt really aggrieved. It wasn't his fault Hentoff was dead.

"Hmm," said Foxglove.

"The instructions . . ." began Baron, self-righteously.

"I know the instructions," snapped Foxglove.

He sighed. What was the use? Baron was a plodder. Unimaginative. Strictly a shoe-leather man.

"Is there any more on it, sir?" asked Baron. He added the "sir" because he knew Foxglove. That sort of touch sometimes helped to smooth things over.

"On Hentoff? Special Branch has been following it up. We're staying out of it. Don't want to get into it any deeper."

"Was it suicide?"

"That hasn't been determined," Foxglove stated.

"Oh."

"But I don't think so, Baron," he added, patronizingly.

Foxglove smiled thinly. Baron looked at him, baffled.

"The fifth-floor office he fell from was empty. Up for rent. Apparently the door was open. Hentoff simply walked in, and fell from the window."

"That's funny," said Baron.

"Very funny," said Foxglove, without humor. "A spy walks into a building, takes a lift to an empty office, and jumps into the street below. Or do you believe that?"

"Well . . ." Baron hesitated.

"I don't," said Foxglove.

"The inquest . . ."

"I imagine the inquest will be very bland, and the verdict quite meaningless." said Foxglove. He was not guessing. He knew. "It will not make headlines, I promise you."

"But if it wasn't suicide . . ."

"That's right." Foxglove nodded. "I imagine somebody pushed Hentoff." It was a statement of fact.

Baron frowned. "What was he doing there anyway?"

"Ah," said Foxglove. "Maybe he was keeping an appointment. Maybe somebody had arranged to meet him. You were supposed to know."

"Have we any idea who?" asked Baron, desperately.

"That's not your problem now, Baron," said Foxglove, unkindly. "It just seems a pity that you never saw anyone."

"One thing's certain," said Baron. "Hentoff never

made contact with anybody in the street. I followed him the whole time and there was no one."

"Yes," said Foxglove. "What I'm wondering is who was following you."

Baron was still trying to work that one out when he got back to the duty room.

4

Golly let himself into the flat in Holland Park, and threw the evening paper on the hall table. He'd read most of it, but there was still the crossword to do later.

He could hear Sharon bustling in the kitchen. He went in, and found her chopping tomatoes and cucumber for a salad. Pots were boiling, and the kitchen was steamy.

But she looked good, an apron over her slacks, a smudge on her face, hair untidy. Notwithstanding, she was Sharon.

"Just sit down and relax," she said. "It won't be long," and dove for one saucepan, which was issuing steam.

"I thought we were going out," said Golly. "To the mad Polish place."

She looked up.

"And I decided to cook dinner. Out of my way."

She said it mock severely, but as she brushed past him, he stole a quick kiss and she gave him that Sharon grin.

"Put on the telly," she said.

He went into the living-room, and he thought how lucky he was that Sharon was around.

They had come together almost by accident, and now, for all the world knew, they could be a happily married couple.

He switched on the TV. Sharon heard the sound in the kitchen.

"Anything good?" she called out.

"You must be joking," said Golly. "Women in hairnets and northern pubs."

"There's a spy film later," shouted Sharon. "It might be quite fun."

Fun?

"Do you need any help?" said Golly.

"Put on your slippers," ordered Sharon from her steamy, hot center of operations. She was really being the housewife tonight.

But when she brought in the food, she had taken off the apron, and tidied her hair, and put on some lipstick. Golly felt more hungry for her than for the dinner she had cooked.

Afterward they adjourned to the lounge, which comprised two armchairs on the other side of the living room, and Sharon made a big pot of coffee.

"How was your day?" she asked suddenly. "Busy?"

He shook his head.

"One thing's good," he said. "I got our stand at the toy fair. They confirmed it today."

She was just lighting a cigarette, and offered him one.

"Will you have the new models ready in time?"

"Hope so," he said. "God knows what they're doing at the works."

"It's the Panther?"

"The Panther and the Tiger. Both brand new. Swiveling turret, adjustable gun, open hatch, movable machine gun, the lot."

"You're very clever," said Sharon. She meant, I don't understand anything about your toy tanks, but if it makes you happy, I'm satisfied.

The spy film wasn't very exciting. There were two helicopters in it, but Golly had a sharp eye, and he suspected the film company could afford only one and that it was working double time in the action sequences.

He looked at Sharon, sitting opposite. He loved her very much, but he was wondering when, suddenly,

9

unexpectedly, she might bring up the old question again.

In one way, it didn't seem to matter to her that they weren't married. Most of the time she accepted things as they were. But now and then, perhaps when she was tired or he had to leave her on her own a lot and she had plenty of time to think, she would raise it.

She knew Golly loved her. They were close together. Perhaps, in an odd sort of way, it made things even more attractive in bed. And religion bothered neither of them.

But Sharon was a woman. She was committed to him. Golly wondered if she resented that there was just this one part of him she couldn't have.

"You're bored," Sharon suddenly said.

He looked up. She smiled at him.

"You looked really bored then," she said. "I'm sorry, darling. Would you rather have gone out tonight?"

"Of course not," said Golly. He grinned. "I adore eighteen-year-old spy films."

"Do you want to do something?" she asked.

"Yes," said Golly and his eyes took in her sweater, and what was underneath. "I want to go to bed."

They were undressing in the bedroom when Sharon suddenly said, "Oh, Michael, I forgot. Somebody called you today."

"Who was it?"

"I don't know." She unhooked her bra. "He didn't say."

All at once, Golly felt uneasy.

"What do you mean, he didn't say?"

She stood, beautiful and naked, but he had the beginnings of fear in him.

"He phoned twice. Asked for you. Both times when I said you weren't in, the receiver went click. I thought he was very rude."

"No idea who it was?" he said, insistently. He didn't want her to realize how important it could be.

"Maybe he'll call again," said Sharon as she got into

bed. "I wouldn't worry. Can't be anybody important, can it?"

They made love, but the joy had been taken out of Golly's desire, and what should have been pleasure became rather perfunctory.

Sharon clung to him. She didn't seem to notice, but Golly was full of apprehension.

Because he dreaded what that phone call might mean.

5

The inquest on Hentoff lasted sixteen minutes. It was sandwiched between a drunk who had been knocked down and killed by a bus in Shaftesbury Avenue and a sprightly lady of eighty-three who finally died after slipping in the Burlington Arcade and breaking her hip.

The coroner had all the known facts before him. They didn't amount to much. Hentoff had fallen from the fifth floor? Yes, sir. Any indication of how it happened? No, sir. Did you find a note? No, sir. Is there any suggestion of foul play? Not that we can discover, sir.

Then there was evidence that Hentoff, a travel agent with offices in Clifford Street, had been in good health. He appeared to have no financial worries. He was single. There were no grounds to think he might have contemplated taking his own life.

The case is something of a mystery, summarized the coroner. No reason had been provided why Hentoff had gone to the empty office on the fifth floor. Perhaps he had been looking for new premises. Perhaps he wanted to see what the view was like, leaned out of the window, and overbalanced.

On a bench at the back, Foxglove sat and allowed himself his cold smile.

It seems unlikely, said the coroner, that the man had intended to commit suicide. Equally, the police had found nothing to indicate that anything sinister had taken place.

"In the circumstances," said the coroner, picking up his pen, "I shall record an open verdict."

It caused no excitement in court. The press had never heard of Hentoff. The man from Special Branch made a note in his file, closed it, put it in his briefcase, and zipped it shut. Foxglove nodded to Baron, and they both got up.

Outside, Baron said, "Well, that's that, then."

"Is it?" Foxglove sniffed.

"One enemy agent less," said Baron, without sentiment.

"Somebody will miss him," murmured Foxglove. God, he thought, Baron really was second league.

"Sir?"

"I said, somebody will miss him."

"Well, we won't, that's for sure," said Baron, heartily.

"You might not," said Foxglove.

Baron peered at him, but the sharp-nosed face didn't have a flicker of expression. Ah, well, humor the old boy. He likes talking in riddles.

"I'll go back, then," said Baron.

Foxglove looked at his watch. He nodded.

"You do that." There was time to have lunch at the club.

One man he wouldn't invite was Baron. Never.

"See you later, sir," said Baron.

Unfortunately, thought Foxglove.

Over lunch, he wondered who Central might send to replace Hentoff.

6

Both the London evening papers used the Press Association version as it had gone out on the wire:

DEATH FALL INQUEST

An open verdict was recorded at today's Westminster inquest on Philip Hentoff, 48, travel agent, of Tregunter Road, Fulham, who was killed instantly when he fell sixty feet from an unoccupied office in Dover Street, W. There was no suggestion of foul play, said police.

7

When it finally came, Golly sensed what it was before he had opened the envelope.

It was a catalogue from a bookseller, as he knew it would be.

"Military and Naval Books," it said, and the hundred and four pages that followed listed secondhand and antiquarian volumes offered for sale.

Golly quickly flipped through. Ah, page 34.

And there, a book was marked.

Item 296. Ayscough, G. L. *Letters from an Officer in the Guards to his Friend in England.* Half title, 234 pp, 8vo, original binding. London 1778.

Offered at a mere £20.

It was the alert.

"You will get a catalogue of old books in the post. On page 34 a volume will be marked in red ink."

That was the arrangement.

The catalogue itself meant no more than a signal. Marking a book on page 34 was the safety check. Just to make sure. They were always worried about safety checks.

Golly slowly put the catalogue down.

So it was happening. After all these years.

He felt slightly sick. Because it had been such a long time, he had almost begun to live with the hope that they would never bother with him. That they didn't need him.

That, maybe, they had forgotten about him.

Then he would tell himself what he knew to be true: they never forgot.

"Mike, you'll be late."

Sharon's voice came through the bedroom door.

"It's all right," he said.

Funny. His voice sounded normal. As if nothing at all had happened.

"Any post?" called out Sharon.

"Only a bit of bumph for me."

Yes, quite normal.

"I still haven't had that letter from Mother," said Sharon. "She posted it four days ago."

In the bathroom, he stared at himself in the mirror. The gray eyes. The familiar, friendly face. Betraying nothing. Revealing nothing. The laugh lines at the corners of the eyes, and the mouth.

Of course, the catalogue was only the alert. The orange light. All it meant was, be ready for us.

The two phone calls Sharon had mentioned came flooding back. Of course. All part of the net.

When he left, Sharon kissed him full on the mouth. Her lips were warm, soft.

"Are you going to be late?" she asked.

"I don't know," he said.

Grimly, he thought: I really don't know.

8

How they would actually approach him, he had no idea. Or where, or when.

It had been left vague. Once the catalogue came, the contact might appear anywhere, any time.

"Just carry on as normal. We know where to find you. We'll be closer than you think." The colonel had smiled confidently and offered him an American cigarette. All the instructors seemed to smoke American cigarettes. "Leave it all to us."

Would it be a phone call? A letter? A man? A woman? At the flat? In the office? On a bus? In the street?

And he wondered what they wanted him for? After seven years? One thing he knew, they wouldn't make use of him lightly. Having gone to all this trouble for so long, they wouldn't activate him for some little routine assignment. But what would he have to do? Could he still do it?

The sun shone, but Golly felt grey inside. Life had turned sour. He knew it was all inevitable, but the little world he had built around him was suddenly very attractive. And now it looked as if it might be blown sky-high.

He thought of Sharon. She had no idea. Sometimes, in their intimacy, there were moments when he wanted to tell her. She wouldn't betray him. Not Sharon. But he was too afraid. It wasn't really the risk he feared. It was the thought of Sharon's reaction when she found out that he was a lie.

That was why, of course, they couldn't marry. He said he had a wife in New York.

"Divorce her," said Sharon.

"It's no good," he said. "She won't give me one."

"She's got enough grounds, hasn't she?"

"That's not the point." He sighed. "She just won't."

And Sharon had accepted it. They started living together, and the shadow of the wife appeared only at unexpected moments. When Sharon felt vulnerable, or insecure.

Golly suspected that, deep in her heart, she hoped that one day the wife would disappear. Drop dead. Vanish. Get out of their life.

How could he tell her there was no wife? That the reason he couldn't marry her was a quite different one?

15

The catalogue had made him jumpy. He realized that when, in the middle of the day, he called the flat and then didn't know what to say. Sharon was in and was pleased to hear him.

"What a nice surprise," she said. "Are you asking for a date?"

"Of course," he replied. He tried to sound casual when he came to the real reason. "Has anybody called? Any messages?"

"Don't think so," she said, infuriatingly. "Not while I've been in."

"Did you go out then?"

He didn't usually cross-examine her.

"I went shopping. And met Margaret for a coffee. Why? Are you expecting something important?"

"Oh no," he lied. "Just wondered."

"Well, if anybody phones, I'll tell them you'll be home tonight."

"Not to worry," he said.

"I've got lamb chops," she said.

"That's nice."

"Unless you want to go out . . . they'll keep." Her voice sounded inviting.

He didn't know what to say. He couldn't think. He didn't want to make plans.

"Let's play it by ear," said Golly.

"All right," said Sharon. "See you later."

9

For three days he waited, and nothing happened. Obviously, they would contact him, but there was no telling exactly when.

He tried hard not to make it appear that he was watching out for something. In the morning, first thing, he'd go into the hall to see if the mail had come.

The second time, Sharon noticed it.

"You know the postman doesn't come until after nine these days," she said.

16

"Just thought I'd look," he said vaguely.

And when the phone rang, he dove for it. Sharon used to answer it, but now he always beat her to it.

"Who's the girl friend?" she asked after one wrong number.

"What are you talking about?" said Golly. He was irritable. He was beginning to feel the strain.

"The way you rush to answer the phone, I start wondering," said Sharon.

Then she saw his face, and burst out laughing.

"I am only joking, you idiot!"

He smiled sheepishly.

Sunday Sharon was going to visit her mother. Golly didn't mind the old lady. She accepted their arrangement without demur, and he felt she actually liked him. But it meant small talk. Social chatter. He couldn't face it.

"Do you mind if I don't come?" he asked Sharon.

"Of course not. Jenny will be there with the baby, and you'll be bored stiff anyway."

She could be very understanding.

"I think I'll go for a walk," said Golly. "Clear my head a bit."

10

Golly wondered if he was being followed. Obviously, they knew all about him and probably had a good idea of his movements. But did they actually shadow him?

He looked around a couple of times, but he didn't notice anybody, and anyway he knew they'd be good, and wouldn't be easy to spot. Especially if you didn't know who you were looking for.

The weather was inviting, and the park was crowded. On the bandstand near the Serpentine, red-coated Guardsmen were playing Gilbert and Sullivan. Golly strolled over. He liked military bands. They fitted in with toy soldiers. One of the deck chairs in the enclosure was free, and he made his way over just as the band finished its number. There was some soporific applause, and the bandmaster, in full parade uniform, saluted.

Golly sat down in the deck chair, and stretched out his legs. He felt lazy, and marvelously anonymous among the nursemaids with the smart Kensington children, and the grey-haired gentlemen with the *Sunday Times*, and the old ladies with Queen Mary toques. The band broke into "Light Cavalry," and Golly closed his eyes.

But he did not sleep. Relaxed as he was, his mind kept coming back to the summons from his masters. How suddenly his life had changed after seven pleasant years. He'd always known that, one day, the debt would have to be paid, but that one day had seemed so far away . . .

There was a roll of drums, and all the bandsmen stood up and played "God Save the Queen." In the enclosure the audience came to its feet, the old gentlemen stiff at attention, and Golly stood quite straight.

He sat down again. Most of the audience was leaving, and the Guardsmen on the bandstand began packing away their instruments.

"You seemed to enjoy that, Mr. Golly," said the man in the deck chair next to him.

He must have sat down while Golly had his eyes closed. He wore a dark-blue blazer and a Westminster tie. His shirt was Jermyn Street. His eyes were unwavering.

Golly played it very cool.

"Yes, I did," he said, and paused. "But I'm afraid . . ."

"You don't know me," said the man pleasantly. "Of course not. How rude of me. My name is Chance. John Chance."

So this was the contact?

"How do you do," said Golly very correctly. Two perfect English gentlemen, the pair of them. "Have we—have we met somewhere?"

"I don't think so," said John Chance, and gave Golly

an encouraging smile. "But, actually, I know you rather well."

On the bandstand, the Guardsmen were dismantling the glockenspiel. An Army truck had drawn up on the roadway near the enclosure, and the soldiers were loading instruments into it.

Golly felt very uneasy. Something was wrong.

"Let me put you in the picture," said Chance. "I'm from the uh, Ministry of Defence."

Suddenly, Golly's hands felt very cold.

"In a manner of speaking, that is," went on Chance, almost apologetically. "Actually, it's a special department. Security."

Golly said nothing. He just stared at the man.

"Look here," said Chance, "I could do with a cup of tea. Shall we get some?"

He stood up.

"Why not?" said Golly.

11

"We'll have tea for two," said Chance to the lugubrious waiter. "Sandwiches, the lot."

Golly sat in the genteel, faded grandeur and waited. On the way to the Ritz, Chance had talked a lot but said nothing, which had already given Golly enough to think about.

"This is one of the last strongholds," said Chance, looking around amid the discreet tinkling of teacups. "If this one falls, we've had it."

Golly eyed Chance across the table, and gave him a stop-playing-games-with-me look. You've hooked me. Now reel me in. Get on with it.

"Yes," said Chance, as if he had read his expression. "I must tell you what this is all about."

He paused, smiling at Golly.

"What it boils down to, Mr. Golly, is that the game is up. We know all about you."

He stopped, like a chess player who has opened with his king's pawn.

"I don't know what—what exactly you're trying to say," murmured Golly. "What game?"

Chance nodded. King's pawn to king's pawn. Very orthodox reply.

"We've known all about you from the very start," said Chance. "For the last seven years, in fact."

The waiter put down the plate of sandwiches mournfully, and the silver teapot and water jug. Then he shuffled away to another funeral.

"I'll pour, shall I?" asked Chance, and reached for the teapot. "How do you like it, with milk? Or do you prefer Russian tea?"

He said it lightly with his eyes on the teacup.

"Milk," said Golly.

"Oh, that's fine, because we haven't any lemon." Chance nodded and passed him the cup.

He pushed the sugar over, then examined the sandwiches. "Good, two of everything," he said. "But we can swap if there's something you don't like."

"You've known what for seven years?" asked Golly, curtly.

"Everything. They planted you here. As a sleeper. Told you to do nothing but sleep. Until some day when they would wake you up."

Chance selected a chopped-egg sandwich and munched it with relish. "These and the cucumber ones are my favorites," he said. He looked at Golly. "So you've had a good long sleep. And we thought we wouldn't disturb you. Not until the alarm rings. And it has, hasn't it?"

He indicated the sandwiches.

"Help yourself," he invited.

What had gone wrong, Golly kept asking himself. How had they found out?

"The point of all this is that we're rather interested to know why they want you awake," said Chance.

Golly sipped his tea. The less said, the better. He said nothing.

"We've got a good idea what it might be, of course."

"You know, I'd be interested to know myself," said Golly, with a grin he didn't feel, as if the whole thing were a party game and he was now joining in.

"Isn't the reason Hentoff?" asked Chance.

"Hentoff?" Golly was baffled. "Who's Hentoff?"

Chance examined him shrewdly, as if he was trying to assess whether Golly really didn't know or was merely trying a little bluff.

"Who *was* Hentoff," corrected Chance. "I am afraid Mr. Hentoff now occupies six feet in Hendon cemetery. He died quite recently, not very far from here, as a matter of fact."

"What happened to him?"

"He fell," said Chance. "Or maybe he was pushed."

"What's he got to do with me?" asked Golly.

The tragic waiter appeared with a silver salver full of little pastries.

"Ah," said Chance. He surveyed the array. "Which one would you like?"

Golly shook his head.

"It's part of the set tea," said Chance.

"No, thank you," said Golly.

"If you're sure." He turned his attention to the selection. "I'll have the little eclair—oh, and that strawberry thing."

Sadly, the waiter put them on his plate.

"I think," said Chance, reverting to the agenda, "that they have woken you up to replace Hentoff. I may be wrong, but that's my guess. How does it strike you?"

"I'm enjoying this tea enormously, Mr. Chance, and I love the cucumber sandwiches," said Golly, "but I'm afraid I haven't understood a single thing you've been talking about."

"Call me John," said Chance. "May I call you Michael?"

He carefully wiped his mouth with the napkin.

"Don't make it difficult, Michael. It's so pointless.

I told you we've known for seven years. You surfaced in the United Kingdom on August 25, 1970. You landed at Harwich. On a British passport. You promptly fell asleep, and have been very law-abiding ever since."

Golly said nothing.

"And we've been watching you all the time. Everywhere. We knew about it from the word go. Your phones have been tapped. Your mail's been examined. You went on holiday to Frinton in '71. We were there. You spent two weeks in the Lake District in '73. So did we."

He beamed at Golly.

"You remember the night you first met Sharon? You had just broken off with that blonde. The Danish girl. You went to that ridiculous party in Highgate. Where the bloke fell through the window. Sharon was there. So were we."

Golly shivered a little. Perhaps it was a draft.

"We even knew the signal. Page thirty-four marked in any secondhand book catalogue that would come through the post. We opened the envelope before you did the other day. That's why you and I are having tea together, Michael."

"How did you find out?" said Golly, in a low voice.

"That's naughty," chided Chance. "We're professionals, and professionals don't ask each other that kind of question. Two old ladies don't ask each other how they keep their skin free of wrinkles, do they?"

An American couple came in, looked around and sat down at a table in the corner. The woman had a very big behind and, unfortunately, was wearing trousers.

"There's no style any more." Chance sighed. "Not even at the Ritz."

He poured himself another cup.

"More tea?" he asked. "I'm afraid it's a bit stewed, but I am sure they can get us some more hot water."

"I've had enough," said Golly. He meant it.

"You could be in lots of trouble, actually," said

Chance. "It's all very well being a sleeper, but living a false life with a false identity and using false papers is a serious offense. For starters, as our American friends would say."

"Who says they're false?" challenged Golly.

"I do," said Chance, very quietly.

"I'm legitimate. I manufacture toys. Everything I do is legal."

"I like your toys," said Chance. "That Scorpion thing last Christmas was beautiful, and I loved the little flame thrower."

He sighed.

"But I'm afraid we could put you away. You know that. Certainly ten years. Maybe fifteen. Even twenty. If the Lord Chief has a bad breakfast, it could be thirty. That would be terrible, Michael."

"Oh, no," said Golly. "You can't. I haven't done a thing. Not raised a finger. It's all been perfectly legal, and you know that if you've been watching me. I've been asleep, remember?"

"My dear chap," said Chance. "If we really wanted to, we could put you away now, and you know it. With any section of the Official Secrets Act you care to name. You forget, Mr. Golly, that your whole phony existence only works as long as nobody starts probing."

He sipped his tea.

"What a funny name . . . Golly . . . How did they think of that one? Or did they have a handy passport?"

He smiled coldly.

"Doesn't matter. Don't worry about it, Michael. But believe me, cross us, and your feet won't touch ground again." He paused. "Neither will Sharon's."

"She doesn't know anything," said Golly. Suddenly, he was panicky. "Leave her out of this. She knows nothing."

"Of course not," said Chance. "I know that. You know that. But she'd have a hell of a time proving it.

Think what we might find among her undies if we searched the bedroom. You know what I mean?"

Golly was trying to stop himself from shaking.

"All that's quite stupid," said Chance soothingly. "No need for us even to discuss it. Now that we're all agreed to cards on the table, face upwards."

"What happens to me now?"

"Nothing, Michael," said Chance. "What possibly could happen to you? All we want from you is co-operation. When your masters contact you and give you your assignment, you keep us posted. You tell us all about everything. That's all."

"Tell you everything?"

"Of course." Chance signaled the waiter. "And then do what we say."

He brushed away a crumb from his school tie.

"They haven't actually approached me," said Golly in a low voice.

Chance nodded. "We know that. But they will. Quite soon, I imagine. That's why I thought we'd have this little chat now. So that you know where you stand."

"Maybe they'll think again. Maybe they won't even contact me," said Golly, but he didn't even believe that himself.

"Michael, they haven't woken you up for nothing," said Chance.

The waiter brought a plate with the bill on it. He seemed full of regret. Chance put down some money, and the waiter shuffled away, miserable to the last.

Chance produced a slim wallet and took out a visiting card.

"Here," he said, "you can always reach me at this number. If I'm not there, leave a message. Call me immediately when you hear from your friends."

Golly took the card. It had just a name—J. D. Chance—And a number. No address. No extension.

"And don't try to hold out on us," said Chance, gently. "Please." He was almost sincere. "It would be so unpleasant for you. And quite pointless." He smiled.

"We will know anyway when they contact you. The moment it happens."

"You know what you are asking me to do," said Golly.

"Of course. But you really can't afford scruples, you know. Self-preservation is now the name of the game. And remember one thing—they wouldn't hesitate a moment to ditch you if it were necessary."

He saw the unhappy look on Golly's face.

"You're not alone in this, Michael," he said softly. "You have a friend. Me. You will be able to confide in me, tell me everything, lean on me. You now have somebody to share your secrets with. Isn't that a relief after all these years?"

"You mean, betray everything or else," said Golly bitterly.

"Betrayal is relative," said Chance. "Like the truth."

He stood up.

"Can I drop you anywhere?"

"No thank you," replied Golly. "I'll walk."

Chance nodded, full of understanding.

"Good idea," he said, approvingly. "Clear your head a bit. You must have a lot to think about."

He gave a wave of his hand.

"Call me," he said, and walked off.

Golly kept wondering about the man Hentoff.

He'd jumped, Chance had said. Or been pushed . . .

12

Baron picked up the three buff security folders he had to return to Registry, and then thought he'd try it. Foxglove looked amenable after all.

"Do we know if they've replaced Hentoff?" Baron asked.

Foxglove eyed him with sudden distaste.

"Why?" he inquired.

"I . . . I just wondered," muttered Baron. After all, he was one of the case officers.

"Thinking of putting in for his job?" said Foxglove.

Baron smiled weakly.

"What a funny idea, sir," he said. He didn't really like the joke.

"Isn't it," agreed Foxglove.

"The inquest . . ."

"Yes?" said Foxglove, unhelpfully.

"It didn't come up with anything really, did it? I mean, it didn't explain what he was doing in that building. Or why he went to that office."

"Well, you were supposed to be keeping him under surveillance," said Foxglove. "I suppose if there had been something unusual, you would have noticed it. Wouldn't you?"

Baron wished he'd never reopened the subject. But he wasn't going to be bullied.

"Of course," he said. "Of course I would have. What about the monitoring people? Didn't they pick up anything? Hentoff arranged to meet somebody there . . . he might have done it over the phone . . ."

"Apparently he didn't," snapped Foxglove. "Or they weren't listening when it happened. Or he made the call from a phone box in Leicester Square."

"Leicester Square?" said Baron, with sudden interest. "You really think Leicester Square?"

Give me patience, begged Foxglove. Please, God.

"Only in a manner of speaking. I was citing it as an example."

"I see," said Baron. "Pity. We had him so nicely on a string. Oh, well. You haven't got anything else for me now?"

"No," said Foxglove, thankfully.

"I'm off tomorrow," announced Baron.

"Annual leave?"

"Yes sir. Taking my mother to Bognor."

"Well, I hope you have good weather," said Foxglove. Her Majesty's security, his tone indicated, would not necessarily be totally jeopardized by Baron's temporary absence.

"Of course, if there's any emergency . . ." offered Baron eagerly.

Foxglove nodded. "The duty officer will have your address? Good. Enjoy yourself, Baron."

After Baron had closed the door, Foxglove told himself once again that it was really time the fellow got transferred. There must be a slot somewhere. Atomic energy security. Or maybe naturalization and immigration. There must be somebody who could use Baron.

Foxglove picked up the BBC Digest of Foreign Broadcasts, but then a thought struck him. Baron didn't realize how near he'd come to the truth.

There could indeed be an emergency. At any moment.

Poor old Hentoff, thought Foxglove. He was well out of it.

13

Golly was already in place in New York when they shifted him, and told him to fall asleep in London instead. That was back in the sixties. He knew he had received two promotions in rank since then, but there had been no personal contact with anyone.

In fact, the essence of the operation was that Golly live legally, earning a legitimate living, leading an ordinary life, and he knew no one. Really knew no one.

What they had given him were the two signals. One, the alert, when they wanted him to be ready to be called into wakefulness. The other, his one and only method of contacting Control. To be used only in the gravest emergency. Indeed, never to be used, unless something was very wrong, and everything was at risk.

Even then, he did not know who would be alerted by the panic button. He had no name, no address, no phone number.

"It is better that way," the colonel had said, puffing a Camel. "The less you know, the less risk. Of course, you will have a Control, but his identity does not really matter, does it?"

If catastrophe happened, he could put an advertisement in the personal column of *The Times*.

"Grateful Thanks to Catherine" was all it had to say.

"If we see that, we will be in touch with you immediately," the colonel had promised. "But remember, it means that somebody has to expose himself. That is in itself dangerous. You should only force Control to take that risk if it is absolutely essential. I hope you will never have need to do it."

"So do I," Golly had said fervently, and taken one of the colonel's American cigarettes. They came in diplomatic bags from Washington.

Now the moment had come. He had to warn them.

How the hell had the British got on to him, he wondered. They seemed to have known right from the start, the moment he submerged in England. And they had waited, patiently, cunningly, until he was called to the surface.

Golly knew he was a vital part of the colonel's network. Like the pawn, who does nothing. Until he reaches the last line, and suddenly becomes the most powerful piece on the board.

All right. Now he would play a double game. Let Chance and his masters try to use him. He would cooperate. He had no choice, after all. But he'd make sure that Control knew the situation. And that every time Chance manipulated him, Control would be one move ahead.

Of course, one little voice kept bothering him.

"You're crazy," it said, plaintively. "You've enjoyed life for seven years. Things have been very pleasant for you. You've got Sharon. You've actually dreaded the idea of getting the summons. You just wanted to be left in peace. Now, suddenly, you're planning to play the most dangerous game of all. Why bother?"

Golly didn't want to know the answer. He didn't know if it was a fear of guilt, or a deep-felt loyalty that made him want to warn Control. He knew he wouldn't be able to rationalize it. Guilt about what? Loyalty to what? What was he afraid of, the little voice asked? What do you owe your own masters? Only one thing . . .

"We trust you as we trust no man," the colonel had said. "It will be hard for you, all alone in the wilderness. No one to share your secret, no one to confide in. It may be many years before you hear from us. But when the moment comes, we know we will be able to rely on you . . ."

But he could also hear John Chance's voice:

"Self-preservation, that's the name of the game. *They* wouldn't hesitate a moment to ditch you if it were necessary . . ."

Golly thought hard and long.

And the next day he placed the ad in *The Times*.

14

He knew the reply would come quickly. It seemed a lifetime since he had been in any kind of contact with them, but he knew he could rely on the system.

He wondered if he could tell Sharon anything without giving the whole game away. She knew something was disturbing him, he could sense that. In fact, once she actually came out with it.

"Is anything bothering you, Mike?" she suddenly asked, quite serious.

"Everything." He tried to bluff. "The world, the weather, income tax, inflation."

"No, seriously," she said.

"Isn't that serious enough?" he joked.

"Sometimes I don't think you trust me," she said reproachfully, and his head swung around. He stared at her. What had brought that on?

"What a stupid thing to say," he began.

"Not with anything serious, you don't," she complained. "I'm just a bloody ornament. If something worries you, I want to know."

"Yes, of course," he said.

"I mean it. Or are you trying to hide something from me?"

She looked at him challengingly.

Christ, here we go, he thought. It's come around again.

"If I was your wife . . ."

There was only one thing to do. He reached for her, and kissed her hard. He pressed her body to him, he felt the softness of her breasts against his chest. She made a pretense of unwillingness.

"No, Mike," she said, pushing him away halfheartedly. "It's true."

But he kissed her again, and it all passed.

That night, as she lay asleep beside him, he stared into the darkness with wide-open eyes.

How could he tell her? Sometimes he wondered if it would actually strengthen the bond between them— like a secret that binds conspirators together. But he quickly dismissed the idea. It was as unreal as the thought he'd had so recently—that his masters would never summon him out of oblivion.

Even when he should be asleep, he was awake. The pressures were growing. So was the unease.

And he had a great desire actually to discover them watching him. He knew Chance and his department had him under surveillance. That when he lifted the phone, a spool began to turn somewhere and everything was recorded. That his mail was being opened. Now he wanted to see these mysterious observers.

Sharon caught him lifting the curtains and peering into the street from the living-room window.

"My God," she said, "you're getting like one of those old spinsters, keeping tabs on everybody who goes in and out. Haven't you got anything better to do?"

"I only wanted to have a look at the weather," mumbled Golly.

The morning the ad came out, he hung around the flat.

"Aren't you doing any work this morning?" asked Sharon.

"No, I'm waiting for somebody to get in touch with me," he wanted to say. But all he told her was:

"No rush today. I haven't got an appointment till lunchtime."

"I've got to go out," said Sharon. "I'm sorry, I have to go to the launderette."

"That's all right, love," he said, and sat down with the paper.

He heard her slam the door, armed with her two carrier bags of washing.

And he waited, like a young lover, for the phone to ring.

Only it didn't.

Sharon came back after an hour.

"Somebody must have popped this through the letter box," she said, and held out an envelope.

It was sealed. There was no stamp on it. Typewritten on it was his name. Michael Golly Esq.

"Well, go on, open it," she said.

His heart was beating a little faster. It hadn't taken them long. It was only just after eleven.

"Oh, it's nothing. Just a circular, I think," he said.

He didn't want to open it in front of Sharon.

"It doesn't look like one," she said. Mercifully, she started going into the kitchen.

He ripped open the envelope.

There was no letter inside. No note. Only a ticket.

"Royal Albert Hall," it said. "Professional Boxing. Stalls M. Seat 1636. Enter by door 6."

It was for that evening.

"What is it?" asked Sharon.

She was standing in the doorway, looking at him and the ticket in his hand.

"Oh, it's for me," he stammered. "They wanted to make sure I got it. You know what the post's like."

He quickly put the ticket in his pocket.

"You're being very mysterious," said Sharon. She shrugged. "Listen," she went on, "You sure you're not in for lunch? I've got some sausages."

"No," said Golly. "I'm off."

To her surprise, he kissed her before he left rather as if he were going on a long journey.

15

The fights were due to start at 7:30 P.M. but Golly's cab became stuck in a traffic jam at Knightsbridge, and by the time he arrived at the Albert Hall, the first bout had begun.

Not that he was the only one who was late. As he edged his way to his seat, spectators were still filing in at every entrance, hardly taking notice of the two West Indians earnestly punching away at each other in the ring. They were bottom of the bill, highly unimportant.

Golly didn't take notice of them either. His eyes were on row M. He searched to see if he could spot—whom? He had no idea who Control was. He had tried to imagine the man who was his sole link with Central, his lifeline to the other side, his master. Tall, short? Fat, thin? Tough, or gentle?

Almost automatically, Golly bought a program, and then moved into his seat. On his right, the places were already taken by two burly men smoking cigars.

"Excuse me," apologized Golly, as their knees stuck in him when he squeezed past.

"Don't mind us," said one of them, a trickle of sweat on his florid face.

"Thank you," said Golly politely, and sat down in seat 1636.

On his left, seat 1637 was empty.

Golly glanced around anxiously. People were still coming in continuously. Again and again, someone would seem to be coming towards row M, but then, each time, pass by.

In the ring, the West Indians were pumping blows into one another, without visible result. As the round ended, there was only a scattering of applause. Somebody might have been cleaning the ring or demonstrating carpet sweepers for all the crowd cared.

Round five, said the indicator, and the West Indians went at it again.

"Couldn't swat a bloody fly," said the burly man next to Golly, and chewed his cigar furiously. "Could he?" he asked, nodding at Golly.

"Not very good, are they?" said Golly cautiously, his eyes roving.

The burly man noticed his looks around the hall, and the empty seat next to him.

"Stood you up, has she?" he said sympathetically.

Golly gave a slight grin he didn't feel. "No, I don't think so . . ."

One of the West Indians slipped on the canvas, and the burly man snorted derisively.

"Maybe somebody blew on him," he said to his companion.

But Golly was suddenly wondering about what the burly man had said. *She?* Was he perhaps waiting for a she? Could it be Control was a woman?

Surely not, he said to himself. But the uncertainty only served to underline his worries and his fears.

The West Indians finished their six rounds and departed for their dressing-room, and the bus-conductor jobs that waited for them.

"What a waste of time," said Golly's neighbor. "Call that boxing."

Golly looked at the program. Two heavyweights were climbing into the ring.

"My lords, ladies and gentlemen," announced the man in evening suit, "in the red corner, Alf Barker of Islington. In the blue corner, Roy Uggins, from Bootle. At the weigh-in, Barker . . ."

But Golly lost the rest because the burly man beside him was giving his prefight summation:

"Christ, what a couple of layabouts. Looks like they trained in armchairs."

Golly glanced at his watch. He'd been there twenty minutes already. Still the seat next to him was empty. Maybe Control was sitting somewhere else? Maybe he was watching Golly at this moment, measuring him up, deciding how to approach him?

After all, if Golly didn't know Control, Control didn't know him either. And if Golly was nervous, Control would be doubly so. Because Golly had sent the distress call that something was wrong.

Alf and Roy, lanky and pasty-faced, were shuffling around, snorting and sniffing at each other. Every time Roy hit out, he hit empty air. Every time Alf tried a punch, Roy ducked.

"They're afraid of hurting each other, poor dears," said the burly man.

"Give them a chance, Harry," said his companion.

Alf and Roy continued dancing around the ring, looking fierce, breathing hard, and leaning on each other repeatedly while the referee yelled, "Break!"

In the second round, they almost embraced one another.

"Give him a kiss," urged the burly man unfeelingly. Alf and Roy broke, and both suddenly landed blows, which had no effect at all. The crowd gave a feeble cheer.

"Why don't you slap each other, darlings?" said the burly man, perspiring. "Go on, Alf," he yelled, "give him a good smack. Go on, sock him one, you bloody poove."

Alf and Roy continued dancing about, sniffing hard. Suddenly Roy hit Alf. There was a trickle of blood, and Alf looked at him reproachfully. The referee waved them together. The crowd gave its nearest thing to a roar.

"If they put a couple of girls in there, they'd do better," said the burly man. "Wouldn't they?" he demanded of Golly.

Golly nodded, his eyes on the ring. Roy was spitting

water into a bucket. Alf was getting his cut eye seen to.

Suddenly Golly realized that somebody had sat down in the empty seat next to him. He turned.

The man who had sat down beside him was John Chance.

16

The new round had begun, and Roy and Alf were doing their best to produce a little action. The thud of leather and the snorting from their nostrils and the shuffling of their feet suddenly sounded louder as the crowd waited expectantly for something to happen.

Golly stared at Chance. He didn't know what to say. Chance nodded to him, and gave him a friendly smile.

"Good to see you, Michael," he said, and then concentrated his attention on the boxers.

Golly too was staring at the ring, but his mind was desperately trying to think clearly. Chance was British security. The man sitting next to Golly should be Moscow's Control. Instead, he was British counterintelligence. He was the enemy.

It couldn't be coincidence, of course. But it couldn't be by arrangement either. Unless they knew the signal code.

All right, Golly said to himself. Play it cool. You don't know what's gone wrong. Say nothing. You've decided to have a night at the fights. Nothing wrong with that. Lots of men go to boxing tournaments.

Roy hit out, and the hope of Islington skidded across the ring and fell to the canvas. His lanky frame seemed disinclined to rise too quickly. The referee counted to nine, Alf stayed where he was, the fight was over, the crowd booed. Alf got to his feet and Roy congratulated him, all mates together.

"Bloody daylight robbery," said the burly man, relighting his shredded cigar. He turned to Golly, then saw Chance.

"Oh, you got here," he said jovially to Chance, as if he knew him. "Your friend was sitting on hot bricks looking all over for you. I thought you must be some dolly bird."

"'Fraid not," said Chance, with a smile.

Golly cursed the burly man. He didn't want to have to explain that he was looking for anyone.

"I'm so sorry I was late," said Chance to Golly. "Traffic was very heavy. Was the first fight any good?"

I'm going crazy, thought Golly.

"Not bad seats, these," said Chance. "Anyway, the best I could get at such short notice."

Golly stared at him. Chance looked right back, into his eyes. He was grinning.

"I . . . I don't quite understand," said Golly, weakly.

"Well, it's as good a place to meet as any," said Chance. "You wanted to see me urgently, didn't you?"

They were announcing the next fight, but Golly kept looking at the man next to him. The man he knew as John Chance.

"Don't look so surprised, Michael," said Chance. "After all, I am Control."

17

The next fight was the big one of the evening, which had two full pages in the program devoted to it.

"Finnessy is a very good man," said Chance, looking at the ring. "He's rated number nine. He'll win, all right. The odds are all in his favor."

He turned to Golly.

"Are you enjoying yourself, Michael? I took it for granted you would be a fight fan."

Golly was still trying to sort himself out.

"Can we talk somewhere?" he said, in a low voice.

"What? Leave now?" Chance seemed upset. "This is the main bout."

"I need to talk," said Golly.

"Well, just hang on a minute," said Chance, focused on the ring.

They were two heavyweights, and they didn't seem to like each other. Finnessy hit the other man under the heart, and his opponent bared his teeth and swung at his face. Finnessy blocked it and propelled a vicious left into the man's stomach. The other fighter grunted, hurt.

"I told you he is a dangerous man," said Chance. "Take your eyes off him for one second, and he'll have you."

Golly studied Chance's profile. The Roman nose, the lips with the hint of a sneer, the prominent chin. Yet, in his own way, quite handsome. British intelligence, every inch of him. Yet, could this be Central's man in London? His own Control? In the ranks of British intelligence?

The crowd was roaring, people were stamping their feet. In the ring, Finnessy had turned into a killer, smashing away at the other boxer, who was desperately cowering against the ropes, trying to shield his face with his raised gloves.

But Finnessy kept ripping into him, again and again, relentlessly. The bell was ringing, the referee was trying to get between them, and Finnessy only stopped when the beaten punch bag of a man slowly sank to his knees, bloody and defeated.

There was a pause while the other boxer was helped up, and then the referee took Finnessy's right hand and proclaimed him the winner. The crowd yelled its approval.

"And, ladies and gentlemen, your applause for a gallant loser," called out the man in evening dress, and everybody dutifully applauded the bleeding wreck, who was trying to smile through split lips.

"Good scrap, that," said Chance.

The burly man leaned across Golly and said, "The only fight tonight."

Chance turned to Golly.

"You don't want to stay for the rest, do you?" he asked, as if there were any question about it.

Golly shook his head. They both got up and began to edge their way past the two burly men.

"Don't blame you," said Golly's neighbor. "There's only some rubbish from Hornsey to come."

In the corridor outside, Chance smiled encouragingly at Golly.

"Isn't it nice, Michael, that we already know each other?"

"Yes, indeed," said Golly, carefully.

"It makes everything so much simpler," said Chance. "What a nice surprise, eh?"

They stood in Kensington Gore, and Chance hailed a cab.

"Let's go to my place," he said.

Before they got into the taxi, Golly saw him give a searching glance around. And after they were in the cab he looked out of the rear window.

He seemed to be very anxious to make sure they weren't being followed.

Then he saw Golly looking at him.

"Force of habit," he said.

Golly nodded.

"One never knows, does one?" murmured Chance.

But once the cab turned at Hyde Park Corner, he sat back and relaxed.

Only Golly found his heart beating a little faster.

18

"Make yourself at home," said Chance in the flat in Swiss Cottage. "Put your feet up."

"Thank you," said Golly.

"Can I get you a drink?"

"Scotch, please."

Chance went into the kitchen, and Golly could hear the refrigerator door opening and shutting.

"Do you want to call Sharon and tell her you won't
be very late," said Chance through the door.

He spoke about Sharon as if he knew her well.

"No, that's all right," said Golly.

He was trying to be very alert. On his guard.

Chance came into the room with the drinks.

He sat down in the armchair opposite Golly and
they both raised their glasses.

"Skoal!" said Chance.

He leaned back and contemplated Golly. He was
smiling.

"Well, Michael?"

Golly was thinking, How do I play this, what is he
expecting?

"What's the problem?" asked Chance, gently.

"I . . ."

Golly didn't quite know how to go on.

"I presume there *is* a problem," said Chance
smoothly, "otherwise you wouldn't have put in the
ad."

"That's right," said Golly. "You're the problem."

Chance shot back in mock amazement.

"I am a problem!" He drank his whisky. "Dear me."
He paused. "Let me put your mind at rest. It's been a
security test, Michael," said Chance. "We had to find
out. I approach you as British intelligence, tell you we
know all about you, put the fear of God in you, and
order you to betray your people and become a double
agent. Obviously you will then do one of two things.
Either you will keep it to yourself and work with the
British. Or you will push the alarm button and warn
us. And that's what you've done."

"I was woken up, right?" said Golly.

Chance nodded.

"Then you came along. British security. Danger. So
I followed procedure. Emergency procedure. And . . .
here we are . . ."

Golly tried to reason it out, a little helpless.

"You mean, here I am," said Chance mischievously.

"Exactly."

"And you wanted to get in touch with me to warn me that the British have compromised you?"

"I—I wanted to get in touch with Control urgently, yes . . ."

Chance beamed.

"Michael," he said, and he was quite solemn, "I am proud of you. I really am proud of you."

"Eh?"

"Don't you see, my dear chap? You've passed with flying colors."

Golly shook his head. "Passed what?"

Chance stood up, began walking up and down.

"Don't you follow, Mike? I had to make sure. Central had to make sure. Seven years is a long time. Things happen. To people. How did I—how did we know that you hadn't—changed?"

Golly said nothing. He just stared.

"Look at it from our point of view," said Chance. "We plant a sleeper. We leave him, submerged, for years. He's human. He leads a normal life. He meets women. He may lose his devotion. He may cease to be dedicated. When he is woken up and summoned to duty, he may no longer be—reliable . . ."

"You don't think," said Golly, "that I . . ."

Chance cut him short.

"We are realists. We understand human frailty. That's what our business is really all about, isn't it? And we have to make sure. Because there is too much at stake."

You look very English, standing there, thought Golly. No blazer this time, just a tweed sports jacket and flannels. And some club tie. Handsewn shoes. Any minute you'll pull out a pipe and start puffing on it.

Yet you are Control?

Chance walked over and grasped Golly's shoulder.

"You're a very fine, loyal man, Michael," he said. "Central will be very pleased. And the colonel will be delighted."

"How's the colonel these days?" asked Golly casually.

"He's switched to Dunhill. He's gone off American cigarettes," said Chance.

He sat down opposite Golly again.

"Yes, it's all a bit of a shock, isn't it?"

"Enough to give one heart failure," said Golly.

Chance's eyes narrowed.

"But you're still not sure? About me?"

"Well . . ."

"The procedure. That is the check, right? The correct procedure. Nobody knows it—except us. That is the safeguard. The only one there is."

Golly nodded. "It's just such a hell of a surprise. First you show up as the British. Now you're my Control."

Chance preened himself a little. "Yes, I think I do make a very good MI5 man. It's the Westminster tie, I believe."

"Did you go to Westminster?" asked Golly.

"Mike, don't ask questions like that. I don't. Who are you? A Russian? A German? You speak German like a native. You sound like an Englishman, but I know in Hoboken you can pass for an American. So what are you?"

"All right," said Golly. He took a deep gulp of Scotch. "I'll only be indiscreet once more. When were you last over?"

Chance shook his head. "Does it matter?"

"Yes. To me. I've been in the desert for seven years. It can get very lonely. Things become blurred."

"Well, you've had a few consolations along the way," said Chance, a little hard. "They've all been very pretty. And you've found Sharon. She's helped to make exile a little more congenial?"

Golly did not react.

"As a matter of fact, we became a little worried about Sharon at one time," said Chance. "Just in case she was making life too congenial. The colonel wondered if you might lose all interest in your real vocation . . ." He raised his hand. "Don't jump at me, that's all past. You've proved yourself, Michael."

41

"I'm glad I haven't let anybody down," said Golly, a little bitterly.

"You never will," said Chance quietly. "Not you."

"You're very sure."

"We're a special breed," said Chance. "We are people apart, you and I. We give up years of our lives, living a lie. But we are dedicated. Nobody will ever understand it. Every country has a few."

He took Golly's glass and his own and went into the kitchen. He was back quickly with fresh drinks. He found Golly looking thoughtfully into space.

"You can relax now, Michael," he said gently.

"You haven't told me one thing," said Golly softly.

"Oh?"

"What's my assignment? You didn't just bring me to life to test me. What have I got to do now?"

"Quite right," said Chance. "There is an assignment for you."

"Well?"

"Any day now."

"What is it?"

Chance paused. "I don't know yet myself. You just stay on alert, ready for orders. You've been woken up, but you can still lie in bed and relax before you have to get dressed."

"Very neat," said Golly, "but I'd like to know more."

"It's safer if we don't," said Chance, and suddenly Golly was afraid.

"Safer . . ."

Chance waved a hand airily. "In a way of speaking. Don't worry."

"What is this thing that could happen?" pressed Golly.

"Forget it for now."

It was an order. Crisp. Authoritative.

"From now on, follow laid-down procedure, as before," said Chance, and he was very much Control. "Carry on as before. Observe the established routine. Don't do anything different. Do not attempt to contact me. I will be in touch with you. Do not approach anyone."

"Who can I approach?" said Golly. "You're Control. The only contact I have."

"Exactly," said Chance. "And remember, you are still half asleep. You've only got one eye open. I'll tell you when it's time to wake up."

He saw Golly to the door.

"Central will be very happy about all this," he said. "No one ever doubted you, but we had to make sure."

"Suppose I hadn't pushed the panic button?"

Chance looked straight into him.

"Then we would have known exactly where we stood, wouldn't we?" he said.

"Good night, John," said Golly.

Chance gave him a wave.

"Take care, Mike," he called out.

Golly shivered a little. The evening had turned chilly.

19

Golly sat in his office, staring at the prototype of the T-64. It was the latest Soviet tank, and the model was going to be the star of his catalogue for Christmas.

It was a beautiful piece of miniature craftsmanship, the replica 122 mm gun with its automatic loader visible through the open hatch, the laser rangefinder, even a tiny fire-control computer.

Golly had taken all the details from the *International Defence Review*, and normally he'd find some amusement in the fact that over here he could pick such information from magazines and textbooks, while in the homeland their mere possession would put one up against the wall.

But today he had other things on his mind.

He was worried about John Chance.

About the whole business.

The trouble was, he had no one he could turn to

for advice. Once he had sent the warning signal, things were supposed to look after themselves. That was his only means of contact.

The procedure had never made allowances for mistrusting Control. One could not check on Control. There was no necessity.

Oh, it would be easy if he could walk into the Embassy and say "I've got a little problem."

But contact with the Embassy was absolutely forbidden. He didn't even know anyone there. And he doubted very much if they had ever heard of him.

"Get out," some frozen-faced official would say. "This is a deliberate provocation. We will ask the English police to remove you."

"But I'm your sleeper," he'd protest as, struggling, he was frogmarched into Kensington Palace Gardens. "I want to check up on something."

He had tried to replay, mentally, the whole conversation with Chance. It was like rerunning a film, trying to spot the continuity mistake you thought you had noticed. But, try as you would, you couldn't find it again.

One half of Golly knew that John Chance was Control. The things he knew only Control could know. It was the kind of trick Control would play. And it made sense that, after all these years, they'd try some sort of test to see where his loyalties lay.

The other half kept being uneasy. Supposing it was a double-double bluff?

He tried to think back to the contingency briefings in the old days. It seemed so long ago.

"Never take a chance," the colonel had told the group. "You will be far from home, isolated. You will have to rely on your own judgment. You only have one policy—no risks."

There were many awkward situations they had trained for. Like explaining a sudden overlapping of dates or some other glaring discrepancy in one's personal story. Like bluffing one's way out of it if the woman one was living with accidentally stumbled across something she should never know.

The one thing they had never discussed was a Control who introduced himself as the enemy.

Suddenly, Golly remembered the visiting card. That's right, when Chance was playing his role of MI5 agent, he had given him his card, with the number to call at any time of day or night. The number where he could always be reached.

That was the number of John Chance, British agent.

Golly took out the card and studied it. He wondered what would happen if he dialed the number. Would some impersonal voice say "Ministry of Defense"? Or would there be sudden stammering and stuttering when he asked for Chance?

Golly pulled the phone toward him. He dialed the number carefully, making sure each digit was correct. He wanted no misrouting.

But there was no ringing tone at the other end. Just a high-pitched buzz.

Golly put the phone down. Waited impatiently. Dialed again. And once more, the buzz.

He dialed 100 and gave the operator the number.

"What seems to be the trouble?" asked the operator, completely disinterested.

"I don't know," said Golly. "I can't make out the sound. It's not engaged. Perhaps you could get it for me."

"One moment."

He heard the dialing at the exchange. And then, again, the same high-pitched buzz.

"Just one moment," said the operator. "I'll check the line."

Within a few seconds she came back to him.

"The number you want is not in use," she said.

"What do you mean, not in use? It's a friend of mine. It's—it's his office."

"I'm sorry," said the operator. "There is no subscriber at this number."

"Since when?" asked Golly.

"I have no idea," said the operator, and she was plainly getting impatient. "Do you have an address?"

"Er . . . no . . ."

"Sorry," said the operator, and the line went dead.

Golly slowly hung up the phone. He reached for the A-D directory. There were fifty-eight Chances in the London area. Nine of them had the initial "J." Not one was "J. D."

But, for the next half hour, Golly was busy ringing all the Chances in the book. And not one of them was his man. Golly ran out of variations of his query—that he was looking for an old school friend from Westminster and he wondered whether, et cetera.

So.

A blank all the way.

Golly scratched his chin, puzzled. When Chance gave him the number in his British intelligence guise, he had no guarantee that Golly would not ring him. After all, in his new-found capacity as double agent, he might have had something urgent to communicate to Chance. So presumably the number worked then.

Only now, after Chance had revealed himself as Control, did it apparently no longer exist. Well, perhaps that all fit. Perhaps Chance had rigged up a phony MI5 number. And canceled it the moment it was no longer needed.

Like everything else about John Chance, it was perfectly possible, and yet . . .

Golly left the office, and knew that what he was about to do was a complete violation of the laid-down procedure of operations.

He was checking into the background of his Control. No one was authorized to do that. It was like opening your commanding officer's mail, or following him to see if he was keeping a secret date with an illicit girl friend.

But, since Golly had no one to turn to, he felt entitled to bend the rules. The more he knew about the suave John Chance, the more secure he would feel.

And the safer.

He took a cab to Swiss Cottage. He remembered the street where Chance lived, and the house was easy to find. He didn't quite know what he would say if he arrived at the flat and Chance demanded an explanation, but he'd deal with that one when he had to.

Golly got out of the cab and paid it off. He mounted the four steps to the front door. The house was divided into flats. There were no names on the bell push, only a number for each flat. John Chance lived in Flat 2. That he also remembered well.

He pushed the bell of No. 2.

Nothing happened.

He tried again.

From the basement, a voice called up to him:

"Yes? Who do you want?"

It was a caretaker, elderly, unshaven, with no tie or collar.

"Mr. Chance," said Golly.

"Who?" The caretaker was puzzled.

"He lives in Flat 2," said Golly.

The caretaker wheezed slowly up the basement steps. He looked at Golly suspiciously.

"There's nobody in Flat 2."

Golly tried to be patient. "Is he out, then?"

"Nobody lives there," said the caretaker. "It's empty."

"That's rubbish. I visited him here," said Golly. "I was in the flat with Mr. Chance."

"You can't have been, mister," said the caretaker. "It's vacant. Has been for months . . ."

Then Golly knew there was no point in arguing.

"Maybe I made a mistake," he said, and slowly came down the steps.

"You sure you got the right place?" said the caretaker. "Maybe it's another house."

"Maybe," said Golly.

He walked slowly to the bus stop, and got a 13 down the Finchley Road.

As they always said, it's more difficult to follow a man when he's traveling by bus.

20

"Precisely how do you people want us to play this?" Woodham asked Foxglove.

Woodham was from Special Branch. He had wavy hair, and Foxglove was sure he used hair cream.

"I'm not sure I follow you," said Foxglove cautiously.

"Technically, the matter is closed," said Woodham, tapping his briefcase. "In one way, that is. In another way, the file is still open."

"I don't see any problem," said Foxglove, stirring his tea. "There's been an inquest, the man is dead and buried. Can't you leave it at that?"

"If you want us to," sulked Woodham.

"It's not for me to tell the police how to spend their time," said Foxglove, "but I would have thought . . ."

"An open verdict doesn't close a case," said Woodham. "It means what it says. The thing is still open. The matter is unresolved."

Foxglove smiled coldly. "I don't imagine the late Mr. Hentoff cares one way or the other, do you?"

"That's not the point, Mr. Foxglove. I have to write something on the progress file. I know that Hentoff was of great interest to your department, and that you were keeping him under surveillance. I don't want to rock any boats, but I have to account to my superiors. I have to write something."

"Try one word," suggested Foxglove. " 'Dead.' "

"It's not quite so simple with our lot," said Woodham.

"You should come and work here, Mr. Woodham," said Foxglove.

The Special Branch man drank his tea. It was tepid.

"No." He shook his head. "I've got an uncomplicated mind. I think I'll stay where I am. Now, about Hentoff . . ."

Foxglove had a disconcerting habit of staring over a person's shoulder when he really didn't want to pursue a topic. He was now staring straight over Woodham's, at a Hogarth reproduction.

Woodham shifted awkwardly.

"Trouble is, police investigation and security considerations are getting into each other's way. If Hentoff had been nobody special . . ."

"Who says he wasn't?"

"Give us some credit," said Woodham, a little hurt. "We're not all idiots on the fourth floor. He was on your No. 1 list, wasn't he? He was so hot that your department did all its own field work on him, carried out its own surveillance. We never touched him. You kept us at a distance. I don't know what exactly you had on him, but he was certainly big . . ."

"That's all guess work," said Foxglove airily.

Woodham let that slip by without comment.

"As I was saying, if he was just an ordinary case, we'd be digging around now. We'd be tearing everything apart. But I don't want to throw any spanner into the proverbial works. That's why I want some guidance . . ."

Foxglove pushed the teacup away. "Tell me, all other things being equal, why would you still be investigating?"

"Because, from a police point of view, the case is unsatisfactory."

"Unsatisfactory?"

"Yes. Very much so. We don't think it was suicide."

"Oh, dear," said Foxglove. "You believe that it was . . ."

"Murder," said Woodham. "That's right. All the indications point that way. Somebody probably pushed Hentoff."

"That's terrible," said Foxglove, without emotion.

"And that's where we are stuck," said Woodham. "We haven't got anything beyond that. No who, no why."

"Well," said Foxglove, "maybe something will come up."

Woodham looked at him hard. "But you'd rather we left things as they are?"

"Let's say, why don't you let us pursue it?" suggested Foxglove softly.

"You think you're on to something?" Woodham leaned forward eagerly.

"We're always on to all sorts of things. You'd be surprised where it sometimes leads us."

"I wouldn't," said Woodham. "We've had too many dealings with you people to be surprised at anything any more. Sometimes it would be nice, of course, to be put in the picture, but I suppose you know best . . ."

"You give us far too much credit for diabolical cunning we haven't got," said Foxglove. "We just plod along, you know."

Like a rattlesnake plods along, thought Woodham. He got up.

"It's been a very useful little chat, Mr. Foxglove," he said.

"If we don't help each other, who will?" murmured Foxglove benignly.

"Absolutely right. And if there's anything new on Hentoff . . ."

"Then, I promise you, I'll let you know. We'll keep you posted on any developments, of course."

"Of course," said Woodham.

They both knew it was a lie.

As he showed Woodham to the door, Foxglove thought he caught a faint whiff of scent.

He uses hair cream, Foxglove decided.

21

Sharon loved sweet peas, and Golly bought a bunch on the way home. He wanted to give them to her as a token of his feelings; to tell her that whatever was pressing on him had nothing to do with her.

She now seemed to have got used to the idea that there were things worrying him of which she had no knowledge. She resented it, but she was prepared to accept it, if he wanted it that way.

He knew it was causing a strain between them, and if it had been anything else—money worries, a business problem, maybe even some woman he had met—he would gradually have brought her up to date.

As it was, Sharon tried to make light of whatever it was that divided them. He appreciated it, and increasingly hated the thing that was shutting her out.

To Sharon, flowers spoke a special language, and he knew she would understand that it was more than a little bunch of color and scent he had brought her.

But when he got home to the flat, Sharon was just emerging from the kitchen with a vase full of green carnations.

"Aren't these beautiful?" she said, delightedly. "Your friend John brought them."

He froze.

"John?" he said stupidly.

"What a nice man," said Sharon. "You never told me about him."

"John Chance?" asked Golly tersely.

"Of course," said Sharon. "He rang, and you were out. He mentioned what an old friend he was of yours, and could he come round and wait."

She ruffled the carnations with one hand.

"Wasn't it kind of him to bring me these?"

"Yes," he said tonelessly. "Very."

Awkwardly, he held out his bunch of sweet peas. They seemed very small compared with the prime carnations.

Sharon put down the vase.

"Oh, how lovely," she said, and gave him a peck on the cheek. "The flat will smell like a garden."

Of course she liked them, but he felt the whole gesture had fallen flat. Bloody John Chance.

"Come on," she said, taking Golly's hand. "Come and say hello to John."

She spoke as if she had known him a long time.

Golly followed her into the living-room. Chance was

sitting on the sofa, reading a newspaper. When they both came in, he got up and gave Golly a beaming smile.

"Michael," he said, his eyes twinkling, "I do hope you won't mind. I have been so wanting to meet your lady, and when she suggested I drop round, I just couldn't resist. Do hope I'm not breaking in on anything."

"Not at all," lied Golly. "Have you had a drink?"

"Sharon's looked after me marvelously," he said, raising a glass. He and she exchanged smiling looks. "What a lovely girl. Where have you been hiding her all this time?"

You bastard, thought Golly. What the hell are you trying on now?

"You're very naughty, Mike," said Sharon. "Fancy not introducing me to John." She turned to Chance. "Do you know, here you are old friends and he never even told me about you."

"Ah, Mike's a crafty one," said Chance, and gave Golly a wink. "I don't blame him. I wouldn't tell anybody about myself either. I'm very boring."

"We'll have to make up for lost time," said Sharon. She was full of gaiety and sparkle.

"It's so lovely to *share* somebody with Mike," she said. "Do you know, I don't think he's introduced me to any of his friends. Sometimes I think he must be ashamed of me."

"Nonsense," said Chance. "I'd keep you hidden away, too. You're far to good-looking to be introduced to all the lechers Mike knows."

"I don't mind being leched after occasionally," said Sharon invitingly. She was on to her liberated-woman thing.

A thought struck her. "Anyway, I didn't know Mike was buddies with a lot of lechers!"

"There's a lot you don't know about our Mike," said Chance genially.

Golly gave him a furious look, but it all seemed to bypass Sharon.

"Now listen," she said. "What shall we do? Are you free for dinner?" She smiled seductively at Chance.

He raised one hand. "Wait a moment," he said. "I just happened to be in the area and, as I haven't seen Mike for ages, I thought I'd pop round. But I'm pushing off now . . ."

"Nonsense," said Sharon. She appealed to Golly. "Shall we all go out somewhere? I could fix us something, but I haven't got much in . . . How about Korski's?"

She saw Chance's questioning glance.

"He's an insane Polish colonel who's got a place at Shepherd's Bush. He kisses every woman's hand like a decrepit Valentino, but the food's super. Isn't it, Mike?"

"If you like Polish food," said Golly reluctantly. Why had Chance come here? Why was he putting on this act?

"I love Polish food," said Chance brightly. "And Russian and Hungarian."

"That's it, then," said Sharon. "Why don't you fix yourselves another drink while I get changed quickly?"

She flashed a bright smile at both of them and left the room.

"Well, Michael, here's to you and that beautiful girl," said Chance, raising his glass.

"What the hell are you playing at?" snapped Golly. "Are you mad or something coming here? What's the idea?"

"We're old friends, relax," said Chance soothingly.

"Now you listen . . ." began Golly, but then the door opened and Sharon reappeared. She was carrying the vase with the green carnations.

"I'll put them near the window," she said. "It was sweet of you, John . . ."

She saw Golly's look.

"I've put yours in the bedroom," she added soothingly. "They're gorgeous."

She turned at the door. "Won't be long."

"Don't get uptight, Mike," said Chance. "It's quite safe . . ."

"This is my place," said Golly. "Sharon isn't part of anything. I want her kept out of it. Here, I lead another life. It's a different scene."

Chance eyed him coldly. "It's the same scene, dear friend," he said. "All the time. And never you forget it."

For a moment, both were silent.

Then Golly said, "Well?"

"Well, what?"

"Why *did* you come here?"

"You've been a little naughty, Michael," said Chance, but he seemed more amused than annoyed.

"Don't talk to me like a fucking schoolboy," snarled Golly.

"Then you shouldn't behave like one. What a stupid thing to do—going to Swiss Cottage. What was the idea?"

Chance waited for the explanation.

"I . . ." began Golly.

"Yes?"

"I don't know," said Golly. "I just wanted to . . ."

He stopped again.

"You wanted to what?"

Chance was patiently boring away at him, like an interrogator under the arc lights.

"Damn it!" burst out Golly. "Put yourself in my position. One minute you're one thing, the next minute another. You change color like a bloody chameleon. First you're from their side, then you're from ours. I wanted to find out . . ."

"And did you?" asked Chance quietly.

"I found out one thing. That flat you took me to—it isn't yours at all. It's a fake. And the phone number you gave me . . ."

Chance frowned. "Phone number?"

"In your MI5 role. Remember? 'Contact me day or night.'"

"Oh, that" said Chance.

"Yes, that," snapped Golly.

"Of course, they're all fronts," said Chance blandly. "You don't think I'd take you to my real home? Lead anybody who is following us to the address of Control? And the phone was just a temporary answering service, so to speak. I'm afraid even I don't have a direct extension to MI5."

"Haven't you?"

Chance smiled. "I don't blame you, Mike, but if you have any questions, you should ask me first. In your own interest. You must protect yourself. You must follow procedure. Always follow procedure."

"I must protect myself against what?" said Golly, warily.

Chance shrugged. "It's a nasty world. And we have a dangerous job. We don't carry guns, and I leave the poisoned pen nibs to the movies, but we mustn't underestimate the risks. We don't want anything to happen to either of us, do we?"

"Like Hentoff?"

It was a stab in the dark, but Chance nodded as if he'd expected it.

"Like poor Hentoff."

"What exactly was he?" asked Golly. "You were very vague about it at the Ritz."

"I don't think so," said Chance. "I said he was dead. That's true. Hentoff was one of us. Quite an important man. And somebody murdered him."

Golly stared at him.

"That's why I said we've got a dangerous job," Chance went on smoothly. "I mean, you don't want to be murdered any more than I do, right?"

Golly's throat was suddenly very dry.

Just then Sharon came in. She had changed not only her clothes, but her make-up. She looked extremely attractive.

"There," she said, "that wasn't too long, was it?"

"You look delightful," said Chance.

"Isn't he charming?" Sharon asked Golly. "I wish you came out with things like that."

"Mike has other good qualities," said Chance magnanimously. "Believe me, Sharon, there's a lot about Mike you probably don't even realize."

22

Korski lived up to his reputation—bowed from the hip when they came in, swooped down low over Sharon's hand, and led them to a table in the corner with great dignity.

He had a rose in his buttonhole, as always, and a floppy bow tie, but he should have been trailing a sabre and wearing cavalry boots with spurs.

"How is *chère madame?*" he said. "How nice to see you."

He clicked his fingers and one of his terrified waitresses came over. They changed at a rapid rate, and always seemed terrified. In the kitchen, Korski's manners were obviously less suave.

He flourished three menus in front of them on which there were a lot of ordinary items you could have in any restaurant, but Korski had added the mysterious words *"à la Polonaise."*

It was a matter of debate among the customers whether Korski's chef was an old Polish general or a Pakistani working from a tattered cookbook. Korski kept that secret to himself.

The food was good that evening, as always, but Golly didn't enjoy the meal. Somehow he felt like a stranger at the table. It was Sharon and John Chance having dinner, and he just happened to have bumped into them. He was the outsider, and they were the couple enjoying themselves.

"What do you do, John?" Sharon asked.

"Whatever pays," he said, and laughed. "No, actually I'm in public relations."

Is that what you usually tell them? wondered Golly.

"Oh," said Sharon. "Huge expense accounts, pretty receptionists and all that?"

"Not really," said Chance.

"Public relations can cover a multitude of sins," chimed in Golly. For no reason, he felt bitchy toward Chance.

Chance nodded. "He's so right. But it makes a living, sort of."

Sharon and he had some beetroot *borscht,* and Golly ate *bigos* as a starter.

Later, Sharon asked, quite innocently, "How long have you two known each other?"

Golly looked at Chance. Well, go on. How long have we, you bastard?

"About ten or eleven years," said Chance. "Isn't that right, Mike?"

"Is it as long as that?" retorted Golly.

"How did you meet then?" she wanted to know.

"Oh, just one of those things," said Chance. "I can't even remember where. Can you, Mike?"

Play your own charade, Golly felt like shouting.

"No," he merely said, mouth full of *bigos.*

"Want to know something funny?" said Chance.

"Go on," said Sharon.

"When I first met him, I didn't actually like him. I thought, Here's an unsociable cuss."

"He's that all right," said Sharon fondly, and gave him a smile.

Here goes, thought Golly.

"I felt the same way about him," he said. "I thought, What a stuck-up snob. Always wearing his old school tie."

Chance beamed at him. *Touché.*

"That isn't a school tie you're wearing now, is it?" asked Sharon, looking at the black necktie with the thin pink stripe.

" 'Fraid so," said Chance. "Westminster."

"I told you," said Golly. "Nothing but a bloody snob. I don't know why I put up with him. Do I, John?"

His grin was cold.

"Neither do I," said Chance. "But I was fond of the

old place. The school of diplomats, actors, and mounte-banks."

"Which group do you fall into?" asked Golly inno-cently, but the frightened waitress brought the wild duck and the *schnitzel à la Polonaise*, and they got busy eating Korski's finest.

Afterward, over coffee, Sharon and John Chance got on like a house afire. They were like two people who have a lot in common—mutual interests, mutual opinions.

Chance made her laugh, and she was really enjoying herself. Only now and then they brought Golly into it, so as not to make him feel too obviously left out.

"Tell me," said Chance, "how did you two actually get together?"

He looked from one to the other expectantly.

"We just met," said Golly. You know bloody well how we got together, he thought.

"Oh, sometimes you're so—unromantic," said Sharon. She turned to Chance. "Actually, he was drunk. He picked me up at a party. He was having a steamy affair with some Scandanavian bird at the time. Poor kid."

She giggled.

"He's a swinger," said Chance. "Our Mike gets around."

"Not now, he doesn't. Do you, Mike?" she added accusingly.

"Don't be stupid," he said, surlily.

"Anyway, what happened then?" asked Chance.

"Well, you know. One thing led to another," she said.

"Yes, I suppose that's when his marriage had just broken up," said Chance, as if they were discussing some absent party.

Are you doing it to show you know my cover story? wondered Golly.

Sharon nodded, didn't say anything.

"Actually, you really came between us," smiled Chance. "Until he met you, we'd get together two, three times a week, get pissed, all boys together. We had a laugh or two, didn't we, Mike?"

"I suppose so," muttered Golly.

"But once he met you, he didn't have time for anyone else. And I'll tell you something."

He paused. Sharon eyed him expectantly. Her eyes were bright.

"I don't blame him, now we've met," said Chance.

For a moment, he and Sharon looked into each other's eyes. And Golly felt a stab inside him.

"More coffee," he called out to the waitress.

Korski brought it himself.

"Did you enjoy the meal?" he asked, like a regimental commander checking the mess.

"It was lovely," said Sharon.

"I'll have to bring some of my friends here," said Chance.

"I hope so," said Korski. "They'll be very welcome, always."

When they decided to leave, there was a ritual *pas de deux* over the bill.

"I insist," said Chance. "After all, I burst in on you and intruded into your evening . . ."

"Nonsense," said Sharon. "You're our guest. Isn't he, Mike?"

"Of course," said Golly. He put down the money.

"Actually, I could put this evening on expenses," said Chance slyly.

I bet, Golly wanted to say.

"You keep that for next time," he said aloud.

"Can we drop John somewhere?" asked Sharon outside, as they looked for a taxi.

"No, no," said Chance. "I'll make my own way."

"Yes," said Golly. "He doesn't live our way. He has a place in Swiss Cottage."

"No, actually I've moved from there, Mike," said Chance smoothly.

They said good-bye on the pavement, and Chance gave Sharon a kiss. A very correct, friendly social kiss on the cheek. But Golly could see she enjoyed it.

"I'll be in touch," he promised, and walked off into the night.

In the cab, Sharon snuggled up to Golly.

"What a nice evening," she said, "and what a lovely man. He really is fun. I wish you'd introduced him sooner."

She sat forward and lit a cigarette.

"You are a bastard, actually," she said. "If he hadn't come round, I might never have met him."

"And that would be a pity, wouldn't it?" asked Golly.

She stared at him in the gloom of the cab.

"Yes," she said, very quietly. "It would."

23

Golly wanted to keep Sharon away from John Chance.

She mustn't get involved in this business, he kept telling himself. She doesn't know anything, and she is not part of it. That's how it must be.

But he knew that wasn't the real reason he wanted to keep the two apart. He could still see the look they gave into each other's eyes. He could see Sharon's slight flush. How she had enjoyed Chance's company.

Look, he kept repeating to himself. You're a dull old stick. John Chance makes a change. He's a new face. Of course she enjoyed meeting him. The kind of boring life we lead, she'd enjoy meeting a greengrocer from Lowestoft. Don't read anything more into it.

And he was worried about the fact that Sharon hadn't mentioned John Chance again. Almost as if it were too delicate a subject.

Then his logic tried to take over. Christ, you are an idiot, it said. If she talked about him a lot, and asked questions, you'd be convinced that she's smitten with him and thinks of nothing but him. When she ignores him and doesn't even bother to mention him again, you read all kinds of ominous implications into it. Like she's hiding her interest in him.

He hated himself for thinking about Sharon like this. If he couldn't trust her . . .

And he realized that it was all part of the strain he was under. He was beginning to be unsure of everything and everyone.

He had to pull himself together.

Maybe it would all resolve itself soon. He was waiting to hear from Chance. And he imagined that the next summons would be his orders. The job for which they had aroused him from his sleep.

Golly refused to speculate what it might be. By the nature of the game, a carefully planted sleeper, who had been in place for over seven years, would not be exposed for some triviality, he knew that.

He wondered if it would bring his existence in England to an end. Or would he be able to submerge into obscurity again and carry on once more, living with Sharon in Holland Park, marketing his toy tanks, and sleeping away with his secret. . . ?

Or did they have something in mind that would make it impossible to resume his quiet life?

Whatever happened, he did not want to lose Sharon. If he had to uproot, he wanted her with him. Wherever he'd have to go . . .

Then came the shock.

He was standing in Tottenham Court Road, at the bus stop across from the Dominion.

The traffic was quite heavy but streaming northward steadily. Golly was just about to jump on his bus when he saw the mini. It was a brown supercharged job.

John Chance was driving it. And sitting next to him, laughing and looking very happy, was Sharon.

24

Golly sat by the window and stared out into the quiet Holland Park street.

Waiting.

He could see the end of the street, where it joined

61

the other road. He had done a lot of thinking and he'd made his decision.

And about ten o'clock he saw the mini.

It drew up at the corner. It was too dark to see the driver, but Golly knew it was John Chance. And he knew that mini.

The door opened, the long legs appeared, and Sharon got out.

She turned to wave to the driver and then started to walk up the street toward the house. Golly hastily got up, went into the kitchen, and switched on the light.

He had a feeling of panic, as if he were about to be caught doing something wrong. He looked round frantically, saw the electric kettle, and began to fill it with water.

He heard the key in the door, and then Sharon came into the kitchen, surprised.

"I didn't expect you to be home yet," she said.

"Not to worry," he said. "I only just got in. Coffee?"

"Please," she said.

She looked very attractive. She had her beige outfit on, and the expensive shoes. She had taken pains to look nice. And she did.

"How was Judy?" he asked and loathed himself. She had told him she was spending the evening with her friend Judy.

"Judy?" Her mind seemed to be far away. "Oh, Judy. Of course. She's fine. Bores the life out of me."

He took the coffee into the living-room.

"I'll just slip into something comfy," said Sharon, and went to the bedroom.

Golly sat, and felt very sad. And unreasonably, stupidly angry.

She came back in, wearing her robe. It hadn't been tied very tightly, and the lace of her bra and the promise of her breasts peeped out of the slit.

She sat down opposite him, and took a sip of coffee.

"That's nice," she said. She gave him a bright smile. "How are things with you, love?"

"All right," he said.

"Only all right?"

"Surviving." How long? he wondered.

"Don't let life get you down, Mike," she said, and sounded very kind.

"Don't worry," he said. "I won't."

He meant it.

"As a matter of fact," he said, "I have to go away. Just for a couple of days."

"Oh?" She was frowning.

"Yes," he said. "Business. In New York."

She put the cup of coffee down, and it seemed to Golly that her hand was shaking slightly.

25

The department's viewing theater was a comfortable place, with ten rows of eight *fauteuils,* and an ashtray between each two seats. One sank into the armchair and, when the lights were low, it was very tempting to have a nap.

Foxglove hadn't really wanted to go to the screening of the classified NATO film about urban terrorism, but he'd put his initial on the memo when it came round. Otherwise everybody would tell him what he had missed. This way he could say, "I've seen it myself, thank you."

Actually, it turned out to be quite boring, and very elementary in its approach. Foxglove found himself nodding, but when the lights came on he had his eyes open and, for all everybody knew, had been intently watching for the last hour. But he hadn't noticed that the film broke twice.

When he got back to his office, the press digest was lying on his desk. Marked in red was the article in the *Sunday Mirror.*

DEAD SPY RIDDLE it was headlined, and the story said:

Britain's Secret Service is trying to solve the puzzle of an East bloc spy who mysteriously fell to his death in the West End recently. An open verdict was recorded at the inquest, but the authorities did not reveal that the dead man, Philip Hentoff, was the subject of inquiries by Whitehall spycatchers.

Fast-living, high-spending Hentoff had his own travel agent's business, and made many trips abroad. He gave lavish parties, and was always surrounded by beautiful women.

The net was closing in on Hentoff at the time of his death, and security men believe they were about to make a major breakthrough. Hentoff is thought to have been a key figure in a British-based spy network.

The CIA is being kept closely informed of British moves in the case. The Prime Minister has also asked to be kept fully briefed.

Foxglove did not indulge in four-letter words, but this was the moment when he could have used a few.

And when his secretary came in and said "Sir Deryck would like to see you," he knew what was in store.

Sir Deryck was Deputy Director, and he liked things to be tidy. As tidy as his desk, which was always empty except for a framed photograph of the lady wife, the inkwell and blotter, and the three telephones.

"Do sit down, Gerald," he told Foxglove, who noticed that this time something else was lying on the desk as well. The photostat of the story in the paper.

"Had a nice weekend?" asked Sir Dercyk without interest. He didn't wait for an answer. He nodded at the photostat before him. "Very distressing."

It wasn't exactly the word Foxglove would have used. Awkward, yes. A nuisance, of course. But distressing?

"We could have done without it, yes," said Foxglove.

"How on earth did they get on to it?"

"You know Fleet Street," said Foxglove.

"Yes, but we can't have leakages like this from our department," said Sir Deryck.

You mean, no mention for you in the next Birthday Honors List if this goes on.

"Maybe it didn't come from our department," said Foxglove.

"Who else could possibly know?"

"Lots of people. The police . . ."

"Special Branch doesn't chatter," said Sir Deryck tartly.

"All right, not Special Branch. But think of the people who've been involved. The coroner's officers. The local CID. The Yard, of course."

Sir Deryck cleared his throat. "Well, somebody talked and we must really do something about it."

"If you read it carefully, you'll find it's largely a well-inspired think piece," said Foxglove. "Hentoff was hardly Don Juan or a tycoon. He took a few people to dinner in the West End. That's all. And we haven't told the CIA a sausage."

Sir Deryck raised an eyebrow. "Haven't we?"

"No sir," said Foxglove. "The file is marked 'No Foreign Eyes.'"

"The rest is true enough," muttered Sir Deryck.

"Has the Prime Minister asked for reports?" asked Foxglove innocently.

"That's not on our level, Gerald," said Sir Deryck, smiling thinly. "I wouldn't know."

"Taken all in all, it's not such a disaster, this story, is it really?"

"I do not like to see our top-secret activities exposed in the popular press," sniffed Sir Deryck. "It could be catastrophic to national security."

"In this case, the other side knows all about it already, so the harm is minimal," said Foxglove soothingly.

"I hope the Director shares your view," said Sir Deryck.

As Foxglove returned to his office, his secretary looked up from her desk.

"Oh, Mr. Foxglove, Mr. Baron just called you. He's back from leave. If there's anything you want him to do . . ."

Great, thought Foxglove in the privacy of his four walls. Great. Baron is back. That's all I needed.

It really wasn't turning into his day.

26

"I'll help you pack," said Sharon.

He was due to catch the noon plane next day from Heathrow.

"There's nothing to pack," said Golly. "I'll only be gone two or three days."

"You know you can't pack," said Sharon. "Everything will be crumpled."

She looked a bit down at the mouth. Golly felt sorry for her.

"I'll be back in no time," he said. "You'll hardly notice it."

She gave him a little smile.

Then she nerved herself up to it.

"Mike, I'd like to come with you."

"But, I tell you, I'm only going for a couple of days. It wouldn't be worth it."

"Please, Mike."

"What could you do in two days with me busy all the time?"

"I've never been to New York," she said.

"We'll go someday," promised Golly. "For a real holiday. We'll do one of those thirty-day round trips."

She stood up, went to the mantlepiece, fiddled around with things. She was restless.

She turned around and faced him.

"Is it Ellen?"

Oh, Christ. The woman he had told her was his wife in New York, who would not give him a divorce.

"Are you going to see Ellen?" pressed Sharon.

"No fear," said Golly.

"Why not?" she snapped. "Don't you think it's about time you had it out with her?"

"Look," he said patiently. "I'll be there for such a short time I wouldn't even have the chance. If it wasn't so important I wouldn't be going at all."

"Aren't we important?" asked Sharon quietly.

He felt trapped, like the squirrel in one of those ridiculous wheels that kept going around and around. They were talking about a ghost. A woman who did not exist. A pretext who was coming between them as though she were alive.

On top of everything else.

"I don't know what's going to happen about Ellen," he said vaguely. "Perhaps one day . . ."

"Perhaps one day she'll die of old age. And then we can both celebrate our freedom—in wheel chairs."

She lit a cigarette, furious.

He went over to her, took both her hands, looked into her eyes.

"Sharon," he said. "Does she matter? Does anybody matter? Except us?"

She buried her head in his shoulder and started sobbing.

He brushed her hair with his lips.

Very gently, he said, "I love you. I love you very much."

"Oh, Mike," said Sharon, and her mascara was awash with tears.

He pulled her over to the couch, and they sat down.

"Now," he said, with a cheerfulness and jollity he didn't feel, "what would you like me to bring back from the States? The Empire State Building? Tiffany's?"

"Just you," she said. "Bring yourself back. Safely. Alive. In one piece."

Suddenly, that unease again. He felt worried.

"Of course. I'll be all right," he said.

"No," she said, and stared at him earnestly. "Watch yourself. It's a dangerous city."

"What are you talking about?" said Golly, surprised. She saw his face, heard the tone of his voice.

"It's a dangerous place, New York," she said again. "People get mugged at every streetcorner. Don't you watch TV? Somebody gets robbed in Central Park every night."

"I won't be walking in Central Park at night," said Golly. "Stop frightening yourself to death."

"All right, Mike," she said lightly. "Just take care." And she kissed him.

She was putting on the coffeepot later when he came into the kitchen and said what he had been planning to say for a long time.

"Incidentally," and he made it sound very casual, "I'll only be away for such a short time there's no need to tell anyone I've gone to the States."

"Okay," she said simply.

"If anybody asks, just say I'll ring them. Take their number. Don't say I'm abroad."

"Does it matter?" she said.

"Of course not, but it saves explanations. People get funny if they think you forgot to tell them you were going. You know the sort of thing."

"Sure, Mike," said Sharon, without much interest.

He was relieved. He had feared she wouldn't accept it so easily. But he still had one thing to do.

"Don't mention it to John Chance," he said.

She turned slowly.

"John Chance?" she said, and her voice was a little cold. "Why on earth should I tell him?"

Damn, he was botching it.

"Well, he—he might show up while I'm gone," said Golly watching every word. "He might ask where I am. I'd just as soon you didn't say."

"Very well, Mike," she said, rather tersely. "I won't tell John Chance. I've got the message. I won't say a word."

It had done something to the warmth between

them. Even in the bedroom he felt that a third, invisible person was present.

John Chance.

And he didn't leave when Golly switched off the light.

27

Golly slept fitfully, and toward 4:00 A.M. he woke up. He glanced at the figure of Sharon beside him. She was breathing evenly, a wisp of hair straggling across her face and moving slightly every time she exhaled.

He didn't need to get up until about eight, and he turned over, determined to have another few hours sleep. But, although he closed his eyes, unconsciousness would not come.

He knew what he had to do in New York, but he was also aware that it was risky.

What choice have I got? he asked himself. What alternative?

And, no matter how hard Golly tried to prevent it, John Chance kept appearing in his mind's vision. Wearing his blue striped shirt, that tie, and the big Swiss watch that had all kinds of dials and second hands. Chance, who seemed so English and was betrayed only by the ruthlessness under his suave urbanity.

Golly wondered what his rank was. The man spoke and acted with the authority of one very much in charge.

Lonsdale had been a major, Able a colonel. But, of course, promotion accumulated while one was serving abroad. It was guesswork, but Golly calculated that Chance ranked with Lonsdale.

He speculated how long Chance had been groomed and prepared for this post. Had he assumed somebody's identity, perhaps that of a person who died as a child long ago, or was he a British renegade? Did they find him in Cambridge, or in a Paris bistro or a

Soho restaurant, many years ago? Or had he been raised since infancy in some far corner of Eastern Europe, speaking English every day, coached and trained and groomed for the moment when he would emerge into the outside world as John Chance?

Nevertheless, Golly was worried. They had never prepared him for this kind of situation, and he had no failsafe machinery to fall back on. He knew he had to check on John Chance.

So New York it had to be.

He lay in bed for another couple of hours and then got up, trying not to disturb Sharon, and padded to the bathroom. Then he went to the kitchen, made himself some coffee, and switched on the radio, low.

He sat there in his pajamas, taking in the familiar surroundings—the blue and white wallpaper, the Dutch hand-painted plate on the wall, the bit by the door where the lino was slightly cracked—and trying not to ask himself how much longer all this would be part of his world.

For he knew one thing as a certainty. Nothing could be the same ever again. Once that catalogue came, it was the beginning of—the end?

"Damn you, no," said Golly. "Before I'm through I'll show you."

But the worst thing of all was his suspicion of Sharon. She had been meeting Chance, he knew that, of course. And that was probably the sum total of it. Meeting him. Having a coffee in Wigmore Street. Driving around Regent's Park. A quiet laugh. Some corny joke. See you sometime.

He could understand if she was attracted to John Chance. He could see the man interesting a woman. He could understand Sharon being bored, liking the idea of seeing a different face, listening to different talk.

And he could see what the colonel would have said. A real lecture in what Sharon would call chauvinistic piggery:

"I warned you, my friend. You cannot afford to become emotionally involved with a woman. Have girl friends while you're abroad, go to bed with them, treat them as playthings. A man must relax. Enjoy them. But don't let them enter your heart. If you get too fond of one, pick up with a prettier one. That way, one will push away the other. Falling in love is an indulgence. Don't indulge."

Smiling, he would offer Golly an American cigarette.

Except that Chance said he smoked Dunhill now. And Chance was the thing Golly couldn't really understand. Why was he making a play for Sharon? Control should not flirt with the girl friends of its agents. Control, too, should have no emotions.

Unless, of course, that was exactly it. John Chance had no emotions. He was flirting with Sharon, taking her out, finding out about her to get his claws even deeper into Golly. He was using her. To give him a firmer hold.

Oh, yes, the colonel would approve.

"Mike, you should have woken me," said Sharon.

She was standing in the doorway of the kitchen, pulling on her dressing gown.

"I heard the radio," she said, "that's what woke me. I had no idea you'd got up."

"Doesn't matter," said Golly. "Here, have some coffee."

She sat down at the kitchen table. He adored her without make-up. Make-up made her much more sophisticated, elegant, beautiful. Without it, she was vulnerable, rather trusting, and very pretty.

"What time do you have to leave?" she asked.

"I don't have to check in at the airport till eleven," he said. "I'll get a cab to pick me up here at 10:15."

"I'll go to the airport with you," she said.

"Please," said Golly.

She looked up. That surprised her. She knew him well. The "Please" was almost a plea.

"Of course I will, love," she said.

He smiled gratefully. He felt he really needed her around. What he had to do in New York made it im-

71

possible, but he wished he could put her in his pocket.

Golly had the knack of looking in on himself from outside, and now he thought, How crazy. Our hero, top secret agent, buried in England by Central for special duties when Moscow needs it, key figure in an espionage net, is sitting in his pajamas, drinking instant coffee and wishing he could take the day off and make lots of love to a woman he cherished, but who didn't even know who he was.

"Send me a card from New York," said Sharon.

"I'll be back before you'd get it," he reassured her. "I'll write it and deliver it in person. How's that?"

She smiled.

"I'll fix you some breakfast," she said.

He heard the morning paper slip into the mailbox.

"I'll get it," he said.

"You finish in the bathroom, and breakfast will be ready," she called out.

He picked up the paper.

One item, on the bottom half of the front page, caught his eye.

SPY MYSTERY it was headed.

There was no official comment in Whitehall last night about reports that MI5 was investigating the death of an alleged Soviet spy.

"We have no knowledge of this" said a Ministry of Defense spokesman.

The man, Philip Hentoff, fell to his death in Mayfair, and a Sunday paper reported that he was an Iron Curtain agent who had been under surveillance by British security.

At a Westminster inquest, an open verdict was recorded. Hentoff, a bachelor, lived a quiet life in South West London.

A neighbor said: "He was very polite, and always said good morning. But he kept to himself."

It was the name Hentoff that made Golly read it

again. He remembered what Chance had called him: "Quite an important man."

And how he had added: "Somebody murdered him."

"Hurry up," came Sharon's voice. "I'm putting the bacon on."

"Won't be a minute," said Golly, folding the paper.

Yes, he'd made the right decision to go to New York.

28

In Building 3 at Heathrow, Sharon stood at his side while he checked in. The airline girl took his ticket and glanced quickly at the American visa in his English passport. The visa he had obtained as soon as he settled in England. It was procedure.

"Always have your travel documents in a state of instant readiness. Where possible, do not wait to obtain visas until you have to make a journey. Be constantly ready to move. You never know when you will receive orders."

Except that this time, he wasn't traveling on orders.

Golly looked at his watch.

"I'll be there just after lunch," he said.

"Look after yourself," said Sharon. She clung to his arm.

"I'll be back before the end of the week," he said. "Don't fret. Keep busy. Do things. Go out with friends."

And that almost stuck in his throat.

"Don't worry about me, I'm going to get fixed up," said Sharon. "Jenny's been pestering me to go and see see her, and I owe Mother a visit."

How about John Chance? he felt like asking.

But they were calling the flight.

He bent down to pick up his briefcase, and then a voice said:

"Madame, what a pleasure!"

Golly looked up. The mad Polish restaurant man was kissing Sharon's hand. Then he saw Golly.

"How wonderful, to see both of you," said Korski.

"What are you doing here?" asked Golly.

"I'm flying to Rome," said Korski.

"You don't fly to Rome from here. This is the transatlantic building," said Golly.

"Of course," said Korski. "I am lost. I have been wandering around like the lost sheep. The porter just told me. Then I met you. So I am happy I'm lost."

"You'd better get over there or you'll miss your plane," said Golly.

Korski shrugged. "I am too old to hurry. I miss it, so I miss it. Then I take the next one."

"No, you'd better go," said Sharon, anxiously.

"Where are you off to, you two nice people. A second honeymoon?"

He leered at them.

"Mike's flying to New York," said Sharon. "I'm not going. He'll only be away a couple of days."

Korski shook his head. "Horrible, New York. All gangsters and Mafia."

He bowed.

"Madame, I leave you both to kiss each other good-bye," he said grandly, and clicked his heels.

"Good-bye," said Golly coldly.

Korski turned once more as he walked away.

"Come and have a reunion dinner at my little estaminet when you return," he said, and waved.

They heard him command a porter:

"Take me to the right building for Rome. I am late."

Golly looked after him as he disappeared down the escalator.

"You didn't have to tell him I was going to New York," he said.

"Oh, Mike," said Sharon irritably, "you're getting quite neurotic. Everybody here's going to America."

"They're not," said Golly. "It could be Australia, Cairo, Nairobi, Israel."

"Does it matter?" said Sharon. "Who cares anyway?"

The second call came for Golly's plane.

"I'd better go through," he said. He put his arms around her and kissed her, and she arched her body against his, like an erotic IOU.

"Take care," said Sharon. "Be careful, love. Watch yourself."

"See you in three days," said Golly, and walked toward immigration.

The man was very casual in his examination of Golly's passport. Golly watched his face, but it betrayed no interest at all.

Pity you'll never know you have just let a spy through, thought Golly.

And he began the long trek along the endless corridor to Gate 29, and the New York jumbo.

29

Private and Confidential
D-Notice

Issued for the Guidance of Editors

Within the last few days reports have appeared in the Press about the death of a man called Philip Hentoff containing speculation about certain security aspects of this case.

It is requested, in the national interest, that such speculation be kept to the minimum and that reference be avoided to any possible activities of the security services.

As has been made clear in the past, any public mention of operational activities or methods of security services clearly comes within the restricted areas and should, in any case, never be published without previous consultation with the D-Notice committee.

In this specific case, it is undesirable to pursue the story or give publicity to any of its aspects.

The D-Notice was issued at 3:15 P.M. and within a quarter of an hour was on the desk of every editor in Fleet Street.

By 4:00 P.M. it was on the Tass wire to Moscow.

By 5:00 P.M., Foxglove was in an evil temper. He had known nothing about the D-Notice until it had been circulating for over an hour.

He knew it was Sir Deryck's handiwork.

And he wished Sir Deryck would keep his aristocratic nose out of things.

He picked up the phone, and asked for the D-Notice admiral at the Ministry of Defense.

Foxglove had known the admiral when he had a spell in the Directorate of Naval Intelligence, and he liked the man.

"So what are you going to tell them when they ring you?" he asked the admiral.

"Will they ring me?" responded the admiral innocently. There had already been three calls.

"Oh, come on, Sidney. It's like a scent of water in the desert for them. It confirms their fondest hopes. What will you say?"

"Quite simple, Gerald," said the admiral. "I don't know a thing. I don't know what it's all about. I was asked to issue the notice for guidance, and that's all."

"Well, next time go and tell Sir Deryck to stuff himself," said Foxglove. "It will make life easier for all of us."

"You mustn't blame him too much," said the admiral. "He just passed on the order. The instructions came from much higher up."

"They're bloody fools," said Foxglove, with feeling. "I can't think of anything more likely to draw Moscow's attention to something than to issue a D-Notice."

"Exactly," agreed the admiral. "I rather got the impression they were well aware of that. Could that perhaps be the object of the exercise?"

They were talking on a scrambler line and the door was shut.

"I don't know," said Foxglove.

"What a familiar line," he heard the admiral say. "I seem to have heard it somewhere. Never mind, Gerald. You owe me lunch at the Savile. Phone when you're free."

"It'll be a pleasure, Sidney," said Foxglove, and hung up.

He got up, went to the window and looked across the Mayfair rooftops.

He was an old hand at the game. He was used to its tensions, and its risks. But he had a feeling this one was getting a bit too dangerous.

New York

30

He stood outside Kahn's Deli on Sixth Avenue and looked in through the window.

He saw a couple of men sitting on stools at the counter, eating sandwiches and drinking coffee out of paper cups. The shelves were crowded with cans of baked beans and tomato soup and chili, and salami sausages hung from hooks.

A baldheaded man was wiping the counter with a dishcloth. He wore a white apron, and his arms were hairy.

It wasn't Kahn. It was a long time since Golly had last seen Kahn, but this man wasn't he.

Golly half decided to go in and have a coffee. He could sit there, and maybe Kahn would appear. Or maybe he could just sit and start becoming a familiar face they wouldn't particularly notice next time he came.

Then he stopped. No. Not yet. Maybe next time Kahn would be serving in person.

Golly started walking toward Central Park. It was seven years since he had been in New York, seven long years. But it had changed a lot less than he had imagined. Steam was still swirling up from the manholes, as always, and the road surfaces had their holes and cracks as he remembered them.

"Walk," commanded the traffic sign, and he crossed Fifty-sixth Street. London suddenly seemed very far away, another planet. Even the car horns honked differently here. When there was a jam, the drivers had a sharper, angrier, curter rhythm.

He stopped at a novelty shop and looked at a transparent toilet seat. Quarters and dimes were sprinkled inside the plastic. It figures, thought Golly. Maybe the toilet paper that goes with it should be blank checks.

The familiar corners and turnings were coming back to him, like an old photo album that one takes down from the shelf to look at snapshots of places and people from long ago.

He turned right opposite the park, and started walking toward Fifth Avenue. Rumpelmeyer's still looked like the transplant it was from a Viennese coffee-klatsch house. It always reminded him of Krantzler's in—wait a second, Berlin? Frankfurt?

He frowned. Some of the past was very blurred.

The Plaza was flying a huge United Nations flag, and Golly speculated which African mini-state was ruining its annual budget keeping its pathetic delegation in a state lavish enough to feed half the tribal population.

A very reactionary thought, an inner voice said. Almost imperialist. Watch it. Don't start getting infected.

"Ideological self-indulgence."

He smiled. He hadn't heard that phrase for a long time.

On Fifth Avenue, he turned around and looked at the people behind him. Not that he thought there was anyone following him. Who could there be? Who knew he was in New York?

In London, he had a shrewd idea what the faceless ones actually looked like. He felt he could spot them. Their very anonymity labeled them. The raincoats. The boring ties. The unspectacular shirts. No conspicuous colors. They looked drab and dull, and they carried the *Daily Telegraph* because it was big and they liked spreading it out in front of them if they happened to find themselves sitting opposite their quarry.

And their cars were boring. Usually British made. Vauxhalls, Leylands. Tinny. No mascots dangling in the window. No eccentricity, ever. Anonymous registrations.

"They are very predictable, really," the colonel had said during one lecture. "Special Branch actually has six foreign-made cars, to fool people. And would you believe it, some idiot Member of Parliament found out about it and asked in their House of Commons why Scotland Yard had bought six foreign cars instead of supporting domestic products! And the wretched minister had to explain that the Yard needed these foreign models for 'certain special duties.' "

The colonel had nodded to the man who was operating the slides, and photographs of six French, German and Swedish cars appeared on the screen.

"That's them," the colonel had said. "It's like taking candy from a child."

But when Golly had been based in New York, he had learned to stay always alert for the American security presence.

Maybe Hoover's ideal FBI agent had been a cleancut young man with short hair, in a button-down shirt and a Brooks Brothers suit. But what Central had found out as a result of the Rosenberg thing and the detection of Able and the two plants at the United Nations and the Air Force captain's arrest and all the other things they lectured Golly about proved one golden rule:

You never quite knew. Cab driver, shoeshine boy, Greenwich Village hippie, Yale student, barman, hustler, you never quite knew. They were professionally unpredictable.

On this trip, though, he didn't have much to worry about, he felt. And he'd be gone so soon the computer would still be digesting his landing card when his departure was being fed into it.

He strolled on and kept looking for Reuben's. He remembered those marvelous huge sandwiches, the Grace Kellys and the Frank Sinatras and the Dean

Martins, each enough to feed two. He looked at the building, but it wasn't there.

"Where's Reuben's?" he asked a nervous little man standing in the doorway of his tobacconist's shop.

"Hey, mister, where have you been?" asked the nervous little man. "They finished years ago."

It was sad. He had often gone there. It changed the city, to find the place vanished.

But at least the big toy store was still there, at the corner of Fifth Avenue.

Golly went in.

31

He went to the display case where they had the model tanks and armored cars and half-tracks. They had some nice French models. And a German personnel carrier that was a beauty.

Then he saw a row of his models. They sold quite well in America, and he knew the export figures, of course, but it gave him a thrill to see his designs here.

He was almost tempted to buy one, just to feel the familiar contours, and turn the carefully molded parts.

But he moved away and wandered through the rest of the store. And, if he had not had so many things on his mind, he would have enjoyed browsing in this fantasy world.

"Put away that gun," said a woman's voice, irritably, and a freckle-faced boy reluctantly handed over a replica submachine gun and sulked.

Golly's eyes followed the gun and took in the others on the stand. The snub-nosed automatics, the six-shooters, the detective specials, and the quick-draw pistols.

All phony, of course. All fakes, whose triggers might click, but whose barrels would never spit out a bullet.

Each one, though, looking so much like the real thing.

Golly had the same queasy feeling, suddenly, that

had overcome him as he looked at a window display of surgical instruments in a medical shop near Harley Street. The menace of the scalpels, the saw, the sharp surgical knives.

Like these guns, they too were just on show, but Golly could suddenly imagine them doing their dispassionate work . . .

Deadly. Final.

Watch it, Michael, he reminded himself. You're starting to see spooks.

He walked out of the toy shop quickly and merged with the crowds on the sidewalk. A clock said 5:00. In London, it would be ten in the evening now. He thought of Sharon. He very much wanted to hear her voice, to talk to her, be reassured that . . .

Be reassured that what?

Golly waved down a yellow cab, and told the driver:

"Algonquin. West Forty-fourth, between Fifth and Sixth."

The driver was a Puerto Rican. His name was José Fernandez and the police department photo on the dashboard flattered him, insofar as he had shaved before it was taken.

The José Fernandez behind the wheel had at least two days' stubble, and he grunted a lot. He grunted when Golly gave the address, he grunted when he failed to beat the lights, and he grunted when a Cadillac shot across his bow.

The meter said $1.20.

"Take one fifty," said Golly.

José Fernandez grunted.

Golly collected his key, and waited for the single elevator that served all floors to come down.

"Seven," he told the white-gloved operator.

In his room, Golly asked for his number in London. He visualized Sharon hearing the phone ring, rushing to it, excited at hearing him from three thousand miles away.

"I'm sorry, the party does not reply," said the international operator. "Do you want to try later?"

Golly looked at his watch. It was now 10:30 in London.

"No, it's all right," he said slowly. He put the receiver down.

He sat on the bed and felt, for some unaccountable reason, very depressed.

Of course, why shouldn't she be out? And, anyway, 10:30 was damn early. She wasn't in bloody purdah, after all.

Yet, curiously, it didn't matter whether it was two hours earlier or later. In himself, he didn't really want to know what might be possible . . .

He got up and switched on the air-conditioning. But it hummed so loudly that the noise filled the room like the engine of a small yacht. Golly switched it off again.

He washed, changed his shirt.

He locked his door and walked to the elevator. He pressed the button.

It was time to see Kahn.

32

He sat on one of the stools in the deli. Kahn was there. He had his back to him, behind the counter. It was definitely Kahn. Golly could see him in the mirror, by the cash register. He wore a shirt patterned with girls in bikinis, and he was sweating under the armpits.

Kahn served the man in the blue denims sitting two stools away, reading the *New York Daily News*, and turned to Golly. Without asking, he placed a glass of water by him.

"Yes?" he asked and started skewering some pastrami on a wooden carving board. He hadn't taken Golly in at all.

"Lox and cream cheese," said Golly.

"On rye?"

"Fine," said Golly.

"Anything to drink?"

"Iced tea."

"Coming up," said Kahn, turning his back again and paring off some smoked salmon for the sandwich.

Golly was watching him. Suddenly Kahn looked up and stared into the mirror at Golly's reflection. Then he went back to making the sandwich.

If he had recognized Golly, he didn't betray the fact.

A policeman came into the deli. He pushed his cap back on his head and sat down.

"What d'you say, Sam?" he asked Kahn.

"Hi, Lew," said Kahn.

The policeman had his gun slung low, and the ammunition clips were spaced around his belt like a sheriff's in the old West. Twelve bullets, as police regulations required.

"Gimme a Coke," said the policeman.

Kahn interrupted making Golly's sandwich, went to the icebox, took out a can of Coke and opened it. He gave it to the cop with a paper cup.

"What's new?" asked the policeman.

"Same old story," said Kahn.

"That's the way it goes," said the cop, and took a long swig.

Kahn went over to Golly and put the sandwich in front of him.

"One lox and cream cheese."

He looked into Golly's eyes, hard, but there was no flicker of expression.

"And an iced tea," said Golly.

"Only got two hands," said Kahn.

The policeman finished his Coke.

"What do I owe you, Sam?" he asked, ritually.

"Forget it, Lew," said Kahn, equally ritually. "It's on the house."

Golly sensed it was the usual routine. He wondered if Kahn did it for every cop on the beat.

"See you," said the cop. He gave a half-glance at Golly and the man in blue denims and walked out.

Kahn disappeared through a little doorway and

emerged again with a glass of iced tea on a saucer. He put it in front of Golly without a word.

The man in blue denims folded over his *Daily News* and threw it on the counter.

"The mayor talks a load of shit," he said to nobody in particular. "Where's my check?"

Kahn pushed a piece of paper nearer him.

"Two dollars ten," he said.

The man put down some money and left.

Golly was the only customer.

Kahn began drying some glasses. He completely ignored Golly.

"Long time, Carl," said Golly.

Kahn stared at him.

"Name's Sam, mister," he said, coldly.

"Of course it is, Carl," said Golly.

Kahn looked around him, both ways, as if to make sure the place was really empty except for the two of them.

"What the hell are you doing here?" he asked, angrily. He had lowered his voice so that even the empty stools would not hear him too clearly. "Are you crazy or something?"

"I need to talk to you," said Golly.

Kahn was furious.

"You know the orders, damn you," he said. "You know the procedure. We've got nothing to do with each other. I've never seen you before. I don't know who the hell you are."

"It's important," said Golly quietly.

Kahn looked at him suspiciously.

"What are you doing in New York? Have they sent you?"

Golly shook his head.

A curvy little blonde in an open-necked shirt and slacks came in. The top three buttons of her shirt were undone and she wasn't wearing a bra.

"Three iced coffees, to go," she said.

"Right away," said Kahn.

He disappeared through the doorway.

The little blonde gave Golly a smile.

"Hot?" she asked. "I'm melting."

Golly nodded. "It's hot, all right," he said.

Kahn appeared with three cardboard containers.

"Your iced coffee," he said. The girl paid and walked out, balancing the three containers.

Kahn faced him.

"I don't want you around, Mike," he said. "You know why."

"I'm in trouble," said Golly.

"That's tough," said Kahn.

"We're all in trouble," said Golly.

Kahn frowned.

"Unless I get something sorted out," added Golly.

"You've got a procedure for an emergency," said Kahn. "Don't involve me. Keep to your territory. You know that's orders."

"Don't keep telling me that's orders," snapped Golly. "There are no orders to cover this situation. That's why I'm here."

Kahn looked around again, uneasily.

"We can't talk here," he said. "Where're you staying?"

"The Algonquin. West Forty-fourth."

Kahn shook his head. "No," he said. He thought for a moment. "Be at the corner of Fifth and West Thirtieth at ten tonight. I'll be there."

"Ten o'clock. All right."

"And don't come back here," said Kahn. "Not ever."

Golly gave a thin smile.

"You make a man feel welcome, Carl," he said "I'll have my bill."

"Don't worry about that," said Kahn. "It's on the house."

"You're getting too generous," said Golly. He slid off the stool. "Be seeing you."

"Watch yourself," said Kahn. His eyes were avoiding Golly. And he really was sweating.

33

Golly had been standing around for five or six minutes when an old, battered Chevrolet pulled up by the pavement. Kahn, behind the wheel, sounded his horn.

"Get in," he said, leaning over and opening the car door for Golly.

As soon as Golly had slid into the passenger seat, Kahn drove on. He didn't say a spare word. No greeting, no apology for keeping him waiting.

At the first red light, Kahn asked, "So what's gone wrong?" He kept staring straight in front of him.

"I have to talk to your Control," said Golly.

The light changed, and Kahn accelerated slightly.

"No way," he said.

"I have to," said Golly.

"I don't even know who it is," said Kahn.

"But you know how to get hold of him."

Kahn shook his head. "You know the system. Only in an emergency."

"That's why," said Golly.

The Chevy bumped as it hit a hole in the road. Kahn didn't say anything.

"Where are we going?" asked Golly.

"Nowhere," said Kahn, gruffly. "I don't want to be seen with you."

"That's fine by me," said Golly. "Just set it up."

Kahn grunted. "You're asking me to take a hell of a risk."

Golly smiled coldly. "You mean, you don't trust me."

For the first time, Kahn turned his head momentarily and gave him a sidelong glance.

"I haven't seen you for seven years," he said. "That's too long to trust anybody."

He came to some road work and turned right.

"The city's falling to pieces," he said.

Golly ignored him.

"You'll have to trust me," he said. "Otherwise, we're all in danger."

"No," said Kahn. "That's not enough. You have to tell me more."

In the distance behind them, they heard a police-car siren.

"No," said Golly.

"What's the matter with your own Control? He's the guy you should contact if you're in trouble."

The siren was coming closer.

"That's the problem," said Golly.

"Huh?"

All right, thought Golly. I might as well. "I'm not sure about my Control. I'm not sure he's genuine."

In the driving mirror, he could see the police car gaining on them, its red dome light turning.

"What are you trying to say?" asked Kahn. He swung the car slightly to one side to let the police car pass.

"Just that," said Golly. "I need a check with Central. I want confirmation that my Control is what he says."

The police car shot past them. Golly caught a glimpse of the officer next to the driver busy writing on his clipboard as they raced toward their call.

"What makes you think he isn't?" asked Kahn, slowing down slightly.

"Lots of things. Including the fact he introduced himself as British intelligence the first time we met."

Again, Kahn glanced at him.

"Well," he said. "Can't you check it out some other way? Why drag me into it? Why come over here?"

"For God's sake, Carl." Golly controlled himself. "Who the hell do I check with? The only link in the chain I've got is my supposed Control. If that breaks, I've got nobody. You know we're not supposed to have any other contact. You know we're one-man operations with only one single outlet."

"That's right," said Kahn. "So what the hell are you doing with me?"

He honked furiously as a cab shot across his path.

"Because I happen to know you. We were specially set up, right? You and I are counterparts. Me in London. You in New York."

"That's something you're supposed to have forgotten long ago," said Kahn. "Remember the colonel."

"Fact remains I've got no one else in the world to turn to, don't you see that?" said Golly, a little desperately. "A sleeper's on his own."

"Right. And I am still asleep," snarled Kahn. "They don't want me yet. And you've got no business to jeopardize me."

He slammed his foot down. The car speeded up.

"Except you may be next," said Golly, very quietly.

Kahn had to brake sharply at another red light.

"Okay. Suppose I break silence. What do I tell my Control?"

"That I must talk to him."

Kahn sniggered unpleasantly. "Oh, sure. You think he'll expose himself to you? Come out of the dark on your say-so? What do you take us for?"

Golly didn't like the way Kahn said "us." As if Golly were a stranger, a suspected intruder.

He thought for a moment.

"Tell him that I need authentication for a man called John Chance. That I have been alerted by Chance and told to stand by. That Chance has been following the procedures. But I'm not sure about him."

"Hmm," said Kahn. "He may want to know more."

Golly nodded.

"Tell him he can see me anywhere, anytime. I'm here at his command."

Kahn pulled the car over to the side of the road. They seemed to have been driving in a circle. Now they were outside a flower shop on Seventh Avenue.

"You'd better get out here," said Kahn.

Golly opened the door.

"I'll see what I can do," said Kahn, and he was not friendly. "I'm not sticking my neck out, I promise you. You may hear. You may not. I wouldn't know."

"You just pass the message," said Golly.

"I don't want you near my place again," said Kahn. "Don't call, don't do anything. Forget I exist. I need twenty-four hours, but don't bug me. This time to-morrow night, go to the Village. There's a chess place on Thompson Street."

"What do you mean, a chess place?"

"It's a chess shop. They sell chessmen. People go there to play games."

It didn't seem to strike Kahn that he'd said something funny.

"So they play games," said Golly. "Then what?"

Kahn shrugged. "I don't know. Walk in. Sit down. Maybe somebody will contact you. Maybe not. That's nothing to do with me. Maybe they'll need more time. Maybe they'll fix another meeting place."

"How will I know?"

"They'll find you. Sometime. Somewhere. Maybe there. Maybe somewhere else. Don't ask for anybody. Nowhere. Don't make inquiries. If anybody wants you, they'll let you know."

He gave Golly a final cold look.

"And keep away from me."

Then he slammed the door.

Golly watched the old car drive off, fast.

He had noticed that, under some oily rag, Kahn had a gun in the glove compartment. Maybe Kahn had wanted him to notice it.

34

And suddenly Golly was afraid. Physically afraid. Nothing had happened. But he felt in danger, and he wanted reassurance that it was only his imagination.

It was an ugly feeling, making him keep away from shadows and badly lit sections of the street. It eased a little when there were people milling about and cars passing and policemen standing at corners.

The first time it hit him was after Kahn had driven

off. He started walking down Seventh Avenue toward Forty-fourth Street. Fourteen blocks was a long walk, but he wanted to tire himself out and close his eyes and sleep and sleep . . .

Then he passed a brightly lit, garish bar. Three black men were standing around, and it seemed to Golly that as he came level with them they stopped talking and looked at him. He walked on, and his neck prickled. He was sure that they were following him, and he wanted to stop and find out but he was afraid.

He walked on faster, and then, at Thirty-fourth Street, two tall, long-limbed girls in micro skirts and tight sweaters came toward him, and their eyes assessed him as they approached.

When he came level, they stopped.

"Hi," said one. She had long false eyelashes, and her nipples showed through her sweater.

"Got a match, honey?" said the other with a slight smile, as if excusing her unoriginal approach.

"I . . ."

Golly felt in his pocket. He had a book of matches there. He pulled it out.

"Here," he said, handing the second one the booklet.

"Aren't you going to light it for her, cutie?" asked the one with the eyelashes, and they both giggled.

"Keep them, I've got lots," said Golly, feeling foolish. All the time he was wondering if the three black men were creeping up on him, if these were decoys, if . . .

"Thanks," said the girl with the cigarette, and they both giggled again and walked on.

Golly was sweating. His nerves were ragged.

He saw a cab and flagged it down.

"The Plaza," he said. He leaned back in the seat, and he knew it wasn't actually fear of New York or of a street mugging that haunted him. It was fear of what he would bring on himself if he weren't careful. From one side. Or the other. He knew he was in deep trouble.

If John Chance was his appointed Control, he would not take kindly to Golly rushing to New York to check on him. Nor would the colonel. Or Central.

And if John Chance was the other side?

Then he was in mortal danger, of course, and fully compromised. John Chance's masters might decide he was becoming too awkward. That he had revealed their penetration of the network and would have to pay the price.

Either way, he felt he could be a marked man.

Golly paid off the cab, walked up the carpeted steps of the Plaza and across the lobby into the Palm Court, where the little quartet was playing Strauss and Lehar.

The place was full of long gowns and women with jewelry and men with gold rings and big cigars and pert waitresses who all looked like Off-Broadway hopefuls.

"Coffee," ordered Golly.

"There's a minimum charge," said the hopeful, apologetically.

"I'll have cheesecake, too," said Golly.

The hopeful smiled, relieved, and went off.

"Land of Smiles" played the quartet, and Golly thought of the last time he'd been in this kind of atmosphere. At the Ritz, in London. With John Chance . . .

The day everything had starting going wrong . . .

The waitress brought his order, and Golly relaxed and let the plushy luxury of his surroundings sink in. The feeling of danger had ebbed. Here nothing could happen.

His watch said 11:25. In London, it would be after 4:00 A.M. In Holland Park it would be quiet. The occasional passing car. A few cabs cruising toward the West End. The launderette across the way would still be open, perhaps a solitary figure watching the dirty clothes spin around. And in his flat, Sharon . . .

Asleep, of course. Untroubled. Unaware. All alone, waiting for him to return. Of course.

He drank his coffee and wondered if he should go to the newsstand and get tomorrow's paper.

Then he saw the sandy-haired man again.

35

He had first noticed him at his hotel when he came down and handed in his key.

The sandy-haired man had been sitting at one of the round tables in the lobby, staring at the elevator and following him with his eyes after he came out.

Golly had noticed him, but without much interest. People often wait in hotel lobbies. They study other people while they wait. Just idle curiosity. Golly had done it himself.

So he hadn't particularly taken in the sandy-haired man. He wore an olive-green suit and a dark-brown tie. And his face was expressionless.

That was the last Golly saw of him.

Now, hours later, he was sitting in the Palm Court, drinking iced tea and studying people again, with the same expressionless face. He didn't seem to be especially interested in Golly.

But Golly recognized him. It was the man's anonymity that worried him. In a crowd, he would probably never have noticed him. Only by himself in the hotel lobby, and now here among the sprinkling of people, did he emerge.

Sheer coincidence, of course, Golly tried to reassure himself. After all, the man hadn't followed him. Golly was sure nobody had shadowed him. He would never have gone to the delicatessen otherwise.

He wondered if he should nod to the man. Acknowledge his existence.

For God's sake, thought Golly, the fellow will think you're crazy. Go home. Get a good night's sleep. You may not get it tomorrow . . .

Golly signaled the waitress, and she brought him the bill. He gave her a dollar tip.

"Thank you, sir," said the hopeful one. She seemed genuinely delighted. Well, maybe they're all stingy misers here and leave tiny tips. Maybe, thought Golly, she needs the money badly. Works here at night. Sits at a typewriter all day. Supports an elderly mother and a two-year-old illegitimate child. And wants to be Ingrid Bergman.

"Good night," said Golly.

He got up, walked across the entrance hall, and stood on the carpeted steps, breathing in the night air.

He walked over to the Pulitzer Fountain. He decided to stroll back to his hotel.

He stopped at the cinema across the street, and had a look at some stills. Then he walked up to the corner of Fifth Avenue.

And he saw the man with the sandy hair. He was standing by the fountain, looking across at Golly. As if he wasn't quite sure which way Golly was going.

Then Golly knew he was being shadowed.

36

He walked down Fifth Avenue, quite fast, and yet trying not to hurry. He didn't want to give the impression he had become aware he was being followed.

He had a great urge to stop and look back to see if the man was still behind him, but that would have been an admission.

He could have jumped into a cab, of course, and been back at the Algonquin in five minutes. But that way he would probably never know for sure. Golly wanted it confirmed. He wanted proof that he was under surveillance.

So he walked.

He came to the big church at the corner of West Fifty-fifth, and from the alcove a soft voice called, "Hi . . ."

For a moment he wasn't quite sure who it was the girl was calling. He stopped.

Out of the darkness of the church entrance came a slim girl in a leather coat. She was black, and she had jazzy earrings.

"Looking for company, honey?" she asked.

The thought flashed through Golly's mind: If I go with her, if I let her take me to her room, I'll give sandy hair a run for his money. I'd love him to have to hang around outside some whore's apartment while I'm inside. Maybe the cops would pick him up. Maybe her neighbors would fix him.

But he resisted the idea. "Not tonight, thanks," he said, sounding very English.

"If you're from England, I'll charge half," she said invitingly. He didn't quite follow whether she meant she'd get a kick out of having an English client or felt it might be a case for charity.

"Some other time," said Golly politely.

"Okay," she said, without rancor. She melted into the darkness of the Presbyterian church again.

It gave Golly the chance for a quick glance behind him. Yes, the man was still following.

He passed a police car parked alongside the curb. The front windows were down, and he could hear the radio calls:

"Unit 55, a 10-13, East Fortieth and Third. Unit 12, please respond to my 10-20. Is there a plain-clothes unit vicinity Union Square . . ."

The two policemen were sitting smoking, relaxed. Golly wished he could make trouble for sandy hair. Tell them he was being dogged by a suspect. Get them to jump out and grab him.

But it was the one thing he couldn't do.

Especially if the man was part of the organization. Perhaps Control . . . No, that wasn't right. The man had been in the lobby before he contacted Kahn. Unless they already knew that he was in New York.

Or unless it was the other side . . .

At Fifty-second Street, he decided he had had enough. He didn't need any more convincing.

He waved down a cab and asked for his hotel.

The sandy-haired man just stood on the pavement and watched Golly's cab disappear toward Forty-fourth Street. He made no attempt to follow. Empty cabs were going by in the same direction, but the man ignored them.

He lit a cigarette. The flame of his lighter illuminated his face. His eyes were very pale, bleached blue.

They were cruel eyes.

37

"How's the weather there?" asked Sharon.

Her voice was so close, she could have been in the room next door.

"Humid," he said. "Sticky."

"Are you having a good time?"

"Not exactly." If she knew how funny that one was.

"Poor Mike. Isn't it going well?"

"It's not a pleasure trip," he said.

"I know, but try to have some fun."

"How are you?" he asked.

"Pottering," she said. "Jogging along."

"Never mind, we'll make up for it." He hoped they could.

"When will you be back?"

If all sorted itself out tonight . . .

Aloud, he said, "A day or two. Not much longer."

"Well, take care."

"Of course." Then, casually, "Have there been any messages?"

"Nothing important," she said.

What about John Chance, he wanted to ask. Has he been in touch? Have you seen him?

"Mike," came her voice, "are you there?"

"Yes."

"I thought we'd been cut off . . ."

"No, it's all right." Pause. "What are you doing today?"

"I don't know. Might go to the pictures."

"I'll be back before you know it," he said.

"Of course."

"I miss you."

"Same here."

"Bye."

"Bye, Mike." And then those two words again. "Take care."

He hung up.

That was in the morning.

The rest of the day he had been very careful. He bought a bracelet for Sharon and left the store by a different door from the one he had entered by. He had doubled on his tracks several times. He spent half an hour in the Museum of Modern Art, strolling around half-deserted galleries. He lost himself in the bustle of lunchtime crowds on Madison. He ate lunch in a small Italian restaurant so cramped that no one could have followed him inside without betraying themselves. He even took a cab ride around Central Park, and there was no car following him.

He was pretty sure he hadn't been tailed. Of the sandy-haired man there was no sign. Not all day. He hadn't been around, Golly was sure of that. And nobody had taken over the role of shadower, he was sure of that, too.

He had been walking around the Village for an hour. He had passed the chess place, glanced casually at the carved figures in the window. There were ivory sets, hand cut, and stark, modern ones, a Napoleonic army of chessmen, and a set whose pieces were naked women, with two Lady Godivas as queens, and Joans of Arc as bishops, which made it rather confusing.

He moved on, wandered about, occasionally stopping to look behind him in a shop window, or crossing a street to give himself, a chance to look back.

And he saw no shadow.

He looked at his watch. It was nearly ten o'clock.

38

"Hugo has arrived in Algiers," said a chalked scrawl on a blackboard fixed to the wall of the emporium. "Walt, Patti's gone to Hymie's," said another. Beneath it, somebody had written "Okay, Don. At her pad."

By the wall were seven or eight tables, each with two chairs and a chess set already laid out. Three of the tables were occupied, and games were in progress. Serious, humorless games. A few people were standing around the three games, watching silently.

Nobody took any notice when Golly walked in. Nobody looked at him.

He made a pretense of examining an Oriental set of chessmen on a counter. He picked up a green pawn and studied it. He wondered if somebody would detach himself from the group around the players and come up to him. But nobody did.

There had been no message from Kahn. Nothing to indicate reaction to Golly's plea. Nothing to suggest a change in plans. So Golly had kept the appointment.

If Kahn's Control wanted him, if Central had word for him, he was here.

Golly walked over to one of the empty tables and sat down at it. He was present and visible. All could see him.

There was an intake of breath from one of the three games. A hand reached out and removed its opponent's queen. The spectators crowded closer.

Golly looked at the black and white armies drawn up on the board in front of him. In the old days, the colonel insisted that they all play chess. It was part of the curriculum. The colonel himself never played. Perhaps he didn't want to risk being beaten by one of his people.

Golly felt impatient. How long was he supposed to sit here? Waiting for . . .

"Maybe somebody will contact you," Kahn had said. "Maybe not."

One thing Golly knew. If he heard no more from them, his life was in danger. He had shown his hand, turned to them in an emergency, and they knew what it was all about. If they decided to ignore him, to have no contact, it meant Central had written him off.

They had to confirm that Chance was his Control, or the enemy. Somewhere, sometime, they had to clear it up. If they still trusted Golly.

If they didn't, he was dead, of course.

A girl came in.

She was dark-haired, wore slacks, and her eyes were hidden behind big, round, owlish dark glasses.

She glanced around, took in the three games in progress and the little audience. Then she looked at Golly. For a moment she seemed to hesitate. Then she came over.

"Want a game?" she asked coolly.

Golly stared at her. This was . . . ?

"Well?" she said, a little impatient.

He nodded. "Fine."

"We'll play for the table money," she said.

She saw he looked puzzled.

"It's fifty cents an hour," she said. "To play here. You lose, you pay, okay?"

"All right," he said.

She had long slim fingers, but not a single ring.

She picked up two pawns, one white, one black, put her hands behind her back, then held them out to Golly, fists clenched.

"Pick," she said.

He touched her left wrist. It was the white pawn.

"You begin," she said.

She opened her shoulder bag and took out a cigarette. She offered him the pack. He shook his head.

"Are you good?"

She asked it coldly, impersonally.

"So so," said Golly. "Are you?"

"You'll find out, won't you," she said.

He did. He found out she was very good.

She played fast, a precise, ruthless game. He had made a safe, traditional opening, and she knew exactly what she was about.

He tried to study her while she had her concentration on the board. He was now conscious of her perfume, faint but very elegant. Her cheekbones were high, her lips inviting. But she was very aloof.

"Your move," she said, pointedly.

He saw what he thought was a good opening, and it seemed to fit in with his cautious probing of her intentions. Only after he had made the move did he realize that she was luring his key pieces into hazarding themselves to her.

She brought out her second knight, and now he saw the increasing danger of her strategy.

She seemed to have no interest in him, only in his game. She hadn't asked him his name or anything personal.

He had taken one of her pawns but it didn't seem to matter to her.

And then, suddenly, he saw that one of his rooks was trapped. And if he covered it, his queen was in peril.

Two men came in, one with a beard, went straight to the empty table next to them, and started to play. No. They were not interested in anyone else.

So it was she? Was she the contact? Was she Control?

"Well?" She was still waiting for him to do something about his rook. Only he knew there was nothing he could do. He was trapped.

"Sorry," he said. He moved his white bishop, a futile gesture of defiance.

She took his rook.

"You should never take a chance," she said, with a chilly smile.

He tried to catch her eyes, but they remained hidden behind those huge black glasses.

"Never take a chance . . ." Just a way of speaking, of course. No more than that. And yet . . .

Suddenly, he saw his opportunity. He moved one pawn up, which opened the line of fire to the bishop, and her queen was hemmed in.

"Well done," she said. It sounded mocking.

Don't patronize me, he thought. Just see how you get out of this one.

She checked his king, but it didn't free her queen.

"All right," she said. She castled, leaving her queen to his revenge.

He took it.

"Sorry about that," he said.

"Don't apologize," she snapped.

She took the offending bishop, but now the game was his. And he went after her.

Fifteen minutes later it was over.

She took out two quarters and laid them on the table.

"Thanks," she said. She got up.

"You going?" he asked. Is this all there was to it?

"You want another game?" she asked.

"I wouldn't mind," said Golly. It really was her move now.

"Okay," she said. "Why don't we play at my place?" The black eyeglasses confronted him.

"If you haven't got anything better to do," she added carelessly.

"Of course not," he said.

There was no point in waiting for anyone else.

39

They grabbed a cruising cab at the corner of Bleecker Street.

She told the driver to take them to East Twenty-seventh, between Park and Lexington. Then she lit another cigarette.

"Maybe we should introduce each other," he said.

She seemed almost disinterested.

"What do they call you?" she asked.

"Michael."

"Michael what?"

"It's a funny name," he said. "Michael Golly."

"Lots of people have funny names," she said.

"I'm from London," he said, pointedly.

She nodded. "I thought you weren't American."

But that was all. No curiosity. No "What do you do?" or "How long have you been in New York?"

Maybe there was a good reason. Maybe she knew it all.

And she still hadn't said a thing about herself.

"So what's your name?" asked Golly.

"Does it matter?"

"I'd like to know," said Golly.

"Sharon," she said.

He gasped.

"What's the matter?" she said.

"Your name is—Sharon," he said, weakly.

"What's so strange about that?" she demanded.

What are they trying to do? an inner voice asked. What charade is this?

He tried to collect himself.

"Nothing," he said. "I just—I know somebody called Sharon."

"So you know somebody else," she said. She didn't seem in the slightest bit curious about her namesake.

The cab pulled up outside a brownstone apartment building, next to an Armenian restaurant. They got out, and Golly paid the cabbie.

She let him in, and they went up to the second floor.

It was a small apartment, one and a half rooms. He knew the kind. The half-room was the kitchen. The other served as sitting room during the day and, when the high rise was let down, as bedroom at night.

"Sit down," she said. "I'll fix you a drink. Vodka or Scotch?"

"Scotch," he said.

Not a bad idea, calling herself Sharon, he thought.

If Kahn's Control had checked up on him, they'd know all about Sharon. And if she was the contact, she wouldn't want to give much away. So why not Sharon?

It was hot in the room.

"I'm sorry the air-conditioning isn't working," she said. "It's a real bastard. Blows in hot air in summer and cold in winter."

It was the first explanation she'd given about anything.

"Well," he said, "cheers."

"Cheers, Michael Golly," she said.

She sat down in the other armchair, and she looked good. Her proportions were right. He knew that, under those slacks, her legs would be quite something. So would the rest of her.

But she seemed to make no attempt to signal recognition.

"Tell me, Sharon," he said, "what do you do?"

"I exist," she said.

"No, I mean, for a living."

She still had the dark glasses on. They were focused on him.

"What do *you* do, Michael Golly?" she asked.

He shrugged.

"Exactly," she said.

She stood up, went to a little three-legged table in the corner, and brought it over. On it was a wooden box. She slid off the lid.

"Set them up," she said.

She saw his look.

"What the hell do you think we're here for?" she asked.

"To play chess," he said, blankly.

"So let's play."

She went into the kitchen, and he heard the door of the bathroom open and shut.

When she came back, he'd set up the rows of chess pieces.

She sat down. She was a little friendlier.

"I'm not keeping you from anything?" she asked.

"There isn't anyone you're supposed to meet, is there?"

"Maybe I've met them," said Golly.

She took off her glasses.

"I'll start, shall I?" she said. "You had white last time."

It was another of her games, fast, cut and thrust, no finesses, no classic gambits. She didn't fence, she rammed a bayonet into the guts. Once, she got up to fix them another drink, but she didn't talk at all.

He tried to get a clue about her from the room, sneaking looks between moves. But there was very little that was personal. No photos. A couple of modern prints on the walls. Some plants by the two rickety windows. A few books on a shelf. A calendar from the Louvre in Paris. A small television set.

The end of the game came quite quickly.

"Mate," she said. He didn't realize until two moves before that how desperate his position was. And then he could do nothing about it.

"You play well," he said. "You play like somebody who's got nothing to lose."

"Maybe I haven't," she said.

"What do you mean?"

"Oh, nothing," she said irritably.

Outside, some clock struck midnight.

"It doesn't strike again until six in the morning," she said.

She studied him.

"When do you go back to London?" she asked.

"Don't know yet. Soon. I'm waiting for a meeting."

"Is it important?" she asked.

"Very."

"I hope it works out for you," she said.

He smiled grimly. "So do I."

"And then it's back to Sharon?"

"Yes," he said quietly.

"Is she good for you?" she asked. "Your Sharon."

"That's a strange thing to say."

"I just wonder," she mused. "Do you trust her?"

"That sounds terribly Victorian," said Golly. "Trust

her! You think women should be kept under lock and key?"

"No, Michael," she said. "I just mean, do you trust her?"

Suddenly he wondered. Was this the beginning of something else?

"I don't understand you," he said.

"Forget it," she said. "I talk a lot of rubbish. Take no notice. What's it got to do with me? I don't even know you."

She stood up.

"Another drink?"

He nodded. One minute he was sure she was the voice of Central, the next . . .

She came back with his third Scotch.

"You often go to that chess place?" he asked.

She shrugged.

"Sometimes."

"Do you meet a lot of people there?" he asked carefully.

"You're trying to say, do I pick up a lot of guys there?" She looked at him mockingly again.

"No, of course not."

"Some crazy dame who's got a yen for fellows who play chess. Is that what you think?"

"Don't be silly," he said.

"Why not? What's wrong with that?"

"That's not what I meant," he said.

"So what did you mean?"

He took a long drink.

"I wondered whether tonight was no accident," he said carefully.

She smiled.

"Michael," she said.

"Yes?"

"How about staying the night?"

40

In the morning she made him a cup of coffee and sat smoking while he drank it. She was obviously waiting for him to leave.

"Will I see you again?" he asked. It wasn't so much that he wanted to, but more an attempt to draw a clue, a hint out of her. For he still did not know what her role was.

"I doubt it," she said. "Do you want to?"

"I'm probably leaving tomorrow or the day after," he said.

"After you've had your important meeting," she said.

"Precisely."

Now, perhaps, was the moment.

"It must be very important, to come especially over for it," she said.

"It is," he said.

"With some big, fat, cigar-smoking tycoon?" Her eyes mocked him again.

"I don't know," said Golly. "Could be with a woman."

There. He waited.

She frowned. "You don't *know*?"

"No idea," he said.

"Funny way of doing business," she said.

He nodded. "It's a sort of funny situation."

"Sounds it."

She looked at her wrist watch. She had kept it on while they were in bed.

"Hate to be unfriendly, Mike," she said, "but I'm going to throw you out now."

Just like that? Nothing else?

"I'm in no hurry," he said.

"You'd better get back to your hotel, hadn't you?" she suggested. "Maybe your meeting is all set up. There could be a message for you."

He tried hard to catch her eyes, but she said it quite idly.

He stood up.

"All right," he said. "I'll go."

She went with him to the door.

"It's been nice knowing you, Mike," she said.

"I enjoyed the game." He smiled.

She made no attempt to kiss him, but he took her and she did not resist.

"Thanks for everything, Sharon," he said.

As he left the apartment, she stood at the half-open door.

He turned around. She was smiling a little.

"I hope it goes well with the tycoon," she said.

"I hope it's a woman," he said, and hurried down the stairs.

Inwardly, he thought: I think it is.

In the street, the sandy-haired man was standing outside the Armenian restaurant.

41

He was studying the menu outside the restaurant and took no notice of Golly.

I could go up to him, thought Golly. I could grab him by his coat and say What the hell are you following me for, and who are you, damn it?

And he would say, I don't know what you're talking about, you're crazy, I'm not following you.

And he would look into Golly's face and smile, and the message would be, You're making a fool of yourself, friend, this isn't the way it's done.

So Golly walked past the restaurant, and the man did not turn his head, and they both played the game by the rules.

There was a Mustang with New Jersey license plates parked a few feet away, and the sandy-haired man walked over, got into it, and sat in the driver's seat. He didn't start the engine.

Golly, at the corner, hailed a cab and told the driver to take him to the hotel.

And as he drove off, the sandy-haired man started up his motor, and stayed behind the cab.

Golly was well aware of it. And the sandy-haired man didn't really seem to care. He knew that Golly was aware of his surveillance.

But he clearly didn't mind.

The cab went along Sixth Avenue, and the Mustang stayed on its tail. Then the cab swung right into West Forty-fourth and pulled up outside the hotel. Golly fully expected the Mustang to stop, too, but the sandy-haired man, without so much as a sideways glance, drove straight on, toward Fifth Avenue.

At the reception desk, Golly asked for his key.

"Seven twenty-five," he said.

The clerk gave him the kind of look you get when you have stayed out all night. Golly was very conscious of his unshaven chin.

"There's a letter for you," said the clerk.

With the green key card, he handed over a white envelope. The address was typewritten, but it had no stamp.

"Michael Golly Esq. c/o the Algonquin Hotel, W. 44th St., NYC" said the envelope.

"When did this come?" asked Golly.

The clerk shook his head.

"I wouldn't know," he said, and turned to answer a ringing phone.

"I just wondered . . ." said Golly, holding the letter.

The clerk cupped his hand over the phone.

"Came by hand, I think," he said, and went back to his phone conversation.

In the elevator, Golly did not open the envelope. Now that he held in his hand what he had been waiting for, he wasn't going to look at it here. He was amused by the way it was addressed. Why "Esq." after his name? To make him feel at home? Observe suburban protocol?

It was very un-American, that's for sure.

111

Once inside the room, he sat on the bed. He found himself turning the envelope over a couple of times, as if that might reveal some secret or other.

Then he slit it open.

Out fell a red ticket.

A single seat for Madison Square Garden. For the circus. That night.

For the Greatest Show on Earth.

Just one seat.

42

The man in the phone booth dropped a dime in the slot and dialed the number.

After a few pulses of the ringing tone, a voice answered.

"Yes?"

"It's me," said the man.

"Well?"

"He'll have picked up the envelope by now."

"Good."

"Do I do anything?"

"Where is he now?"

"Still in the hotel," said the man.

"Resting. He must be tired." The voice chuckled.

"Don't suppose he got much sleep," said the man. "What do you want done?"

"Take it easy," said the voice.

"What about tonight?"

"Follow instructions."

"Okay," said the man.

He hung up.

The dime dropped.

43

He was on his feet, standing stiffly with seventeen thousand other people in the stadium as the "Star Spangled Banner" thundered out of the loudspeaker.

Even the clowns in the ring were standing at attention.

His eyes searched the seats in Section M. His ticket was for row C, the third one up, and several seats were vacant.

The anthem stopped, the crowd cheered, the clowns tumbled and rolled about, and Golly made his way up the few steps to the seat.

Quickly, he tried to size up his neighbors. Three girls on one side, giggling and eating popcorn. A fat woman with a child on the other side.

Golly frowned. It didn't make sense. In his section, there were still empty seats, but none adjoining his.

He sat down. He had a marvelous view of the three rings in front of him, and they all seemed to be bowing and playing in his direction.

A tiny dog chased a huge clown, and the girls beside him shrieked. But the little boy on the other side seemed to have done something naughty, for the fat woman cuffed him.

Golly waved to an attendant, who edged in and sold him a program. The little boy gave Golly a spiteful glare.

Golly's eyes roamed around the huge stadium but, in the sea of faces, it was impossible to distinguish anyone. And who was he looking for anyway?

But this was definitely the seat. He checked the stub. He couldn't understand it.

Hilarious Hi-Jinks by the clowns was followed by Hungarian Masters of Manipulation, who gave way to an Esteemed Equine Exhibition by liberty horses, who were succeeded by Astounding Auto Antics, performed by the clowns again.

And Balance Beyond Belief had the crowd gasping as a Frenchman walked along a thin wire, balancing himself with a loaded pole. Only to be replaced by a Wondrous Wizard on Wheels who did impossible things on ridiculous bicycles.

All the while, Golly looked around, hoping to see something, someone, a signal that would give this meaning.

Horses and elephants were succeeded by twenty-one lions snarling and pawing at a blonde, Nordic-limbed German who faced them contemptuously, cracking a whip and humiliating them with a chair thrust in their faces.

"Excuse me," said a man's voice, and a stranger was standing in the aisle, apologetically holding out his ticket to the fat woman. "I think there has been a mistake."

"These are our seats," said the fat woman, belligerently.

The man was quietly dressed, and wore gold-rimmed spectacles. He had a slightly straggly moustache. And he was very mild-mannered.

"I do believe that's my place," he said diffidently, pointing to the seat next to Golly. But he didn't look at Golly once.

The attendant with the programs came to the rescue. He examined the tickets.

"You're a couple of seats farther down the row," he said to the woman.

"I like it here," said the horrible little boy.

The woman cuffed him.

"You heard the man," she said. She got up, trampling all over Golly's feet, and dragged the boy with her.

The man sidled in quietly and sat down next to Golly. He took no notice at all of his neighbor.

The Nordic hero in the arena was now settling scores with a lion who seemed to have more spirit than the others. Finally the lion knew when he had to give in, and ran off down a wired tunnel leading out of the cage in the arena.

The crowd cheered and applauded the hero, and the clowns reappeared, a Gathering of Giggle Makers. Reinforced by Charming Chuckle Churners, the alumni of the clown college somersaulted and cavorted all over the ring.

Golly sat very quietly. The man loved what he saw,

114

and laughed loudly. When they did their water routine, he applauded enthusiastically.

As the next act was about to take over, he suddenly turned to Golly.

"Have I missed much?" he asked.

"Would you like the program?" asked Golly, and handed it to him.

"That's very kind," said the man. "Which one is this?"

Golly pointed at the name of the act.

The man laughed. " 'Pachyderm Projectile,' what a mouthful."

In the ring, the elephants took up position by the teeter board, ready to shoot their trainer into space.

"Here," said the man, giving the program back to Golly. "Thanks very much."

"Keep it," said Golly.

But the man was already applauding as the trainer was hurled into the air and came down successfully. He clapped like a schoolboy on a treat.

"Ladies and gentlemen," announced the ringmaster," the most dangerous high-wire act now being publicly performed is about to start."

"Ah," said the man with the gold-rimmed glasses.

The elephants marched out, and overhead cables and wires and nets began to be lowered over the heads of the audience.

"Ladies and gentlemen," said the ringmaster, "straight from East Germany, the Ulbrich brothers."

The drums rolled. A hush descended over the huge audience.

The man in the glasses leaned over to Golly.

"They really are quite fantastic, Michael," he said.

Golly's head swung around.

The man shook his head and nodded at the acrobats. "We must watch this," he said. "It's absolutely unbelievable, the risks they take."

The band stopped.

Then the roll of drums began again. The Ulbrichs jumped from one wire to the other, defying gravity.

One slipped, and the whole arena went "AAAhhh." But he saved himself in time to get a wave of applause.

And the drums beat a more sinister, tenser background.

Now they were higher still, and seventeen thousand heads craned upwards. Even Golly, his mind full of other things, found himself watching them.

So he never heard anything.

Madison Square Garden roared as the acrobats successfully jumped fifty feet from one wire to the other, and then, balancing every inch, started to walk down a 90-degree wire stretching to the ground.

They had nearly made it when Golly turned to the man.

He was leaning forward, apparently staring at his feet. There was a small reddish stain on his gray suit, and as Golly looked more closely, and brushed against him, the man, very slowly, toppled over, rather like a drunk about to slide to the floor.

Golly knew he was dead.

44

The awful boy had noticed something was wrong.

"Ma, what's the matter with that man?" he called out, pointing at the slumped figure.

"Shut up," said the fat woman. "Watch the acrobats."

In the ring, the Ulbrich brothers were taking their bows, and the whole crowd roared.

Golly knew the man had been shot.

From where, he had no idea. Probably with a silencer. There had been no bang.

Desperately, Golly tried to work out the direction of the killer.

The girls next to him were still frantically cheering the Ulbrichs.

The people in the row behind didn't seem to have noticed.

Only the damn boy.

"Is he sick, Ma?" he asked.

The woman slapped him.

I have to get away from here, quickly, thought Golly. Before anyone realizes what has happened, and the alarm is given. I have to disappear.

The clowns were back and, after the tension on the wire, their pranks were a relief. People wanted to laugh, and they did, loudly.

"Pardon me," said Golly, rising. He had to get by the slumped man before somebody said something.

He forced his way past the man, pressing against him to make sure he didn't slide right off the seat. Maybe they would think he was dozing. People fall asleep at the movies, in the theater. Why not at a circus?

"Excuse me," said Golly squeezing past the fat woman and the child.

The man with the spectacles still sat slumped, at an odd angle, but people were too caught up with what was going on in the three rings.

Golly hurried down the steps, out of the loggia and away from Section M.

His mouth was dry. His heart was pounding. Golly had a dreadful feeling of mounting panic—he had to get away before they found the dead man. Somewhere, in this crowd, was a killer, with a gun. Perhaps waiting to fire again.

The fear was in Golly that he might also be a target. Perhaps the killer was only waiting to get him at the right moment, when everybody is caught up with an act.

He had to get out fast.

He tried to stop himself running, and realized he had gone into an exit under the public seats, leading straight from the ring. The performers' exit.

Golly found himself in a brightly lit corridor with dressing rooms. Frantically he looked for a way out.

117

Then, around a corner, came a clown. His face a white mask, with a big red gash that was supposed to be his mouth and huge black eye rings. Utterly unrecognizable as a man. His face was like a macabre death mask.

The clown stared at Golly.

"You lost, mister?" asked the clown. The gash hardly moved. The words seemed to come out of a blank face.

"I'm trying to find the exit," said Golly.

"The show isn't over yet," said the mask.

"I—I've got to go," rasped Golly. He could hear cheers and applause from the arena.

"Why don't you see the end of it?" said the mask. "See the whole show."

"No," said Golly. "I can't."

He had only one thought: Get away from this man.

"I'll take you," said the mask, and grabbed his arm in a firm hold.

"No," said Golly.

"This way," said the mask.

Golly swung around and hit the man. Hit him right in that white nothing out of which his eyes gleamed.

The clown staggered, and Golly hit him again. The clown groaned and collapsed.

Golly ran.

He ran around the corner, past a beautiful equestrienne who gave him a startled look and said, "You shouldn't be here. It's dressing rooms."

Then he saw a door marked "Private," opened it and found himself in a huge, cavernous garage filled with cages and caravans. In some of the cages were lions and tigers. Three elephants were chained to a wall, bales of hay in front of them.

Golly ran, and he heard a man yell at him. He ducked behind some trucks and then saw the way out, the ramp that let the vehicles out. He ran along it. He could hear somebody else yell, but now he was out in the open air. He kept running, and then he heard the first sirens and saw the red lights coming toward him along Eighth Avenue.

Only they weren't coming for him, they were going straight to the stadium.

Then, in the distance, there was the different, sinister quavering of the ambulance, but by that time Golly was already in a bar.

"What's your desire?" asked the barman. He had a spotted bow tie.

"Scotch," said Golly. "Make it a double."

Outside, more sirens.

"Must be some trouble at the Garden," said the barman.

"Oh, really?" said Golly. He swallowed the whisky in two gulps.

"Another one?" asked the barman, eying him with respect. Two gulps.

"No thanks," said Golly.

He had enough trouble.

He paid, and walked out into the evening air. He had to think very clearly now.

By the curb ouside the bar stood a battered Chevrolet. Golly recognized it.

Kahn was behind the wheel.

"Michael," called out Kahn.

Golly went over.

"Get in," said Kahn. "Hurry."

Golly slid into the seat next to him.

Without a word, Kahn started the car and they drove off.

Then, for the first time, Golly became aware that there was somebody else in the car, sitting in the back seat.

It was the sandy-haired man with the cruel blue eyes.

45

"You stupid jerk," said Kahn.

He changed gear savagely.

"Who's he?" asked Golly, looking over his shoulder at the sandy-haired man.

"Never mind," said Kahn.

"He's been following me," said Golly.

"That's right," said the sandy-haired man.

"What for?"

"Christ," said Kahn, "you've really blown it, haven't you? If it wasn't for you, it wouldn't have happened."

"Was it Control?" asked Golly.

"Who?" snapped Kahn, swinging the car down a street.

"The man in the stadium. The man who was shot."

"No, it wasn't Control," spat Kahn. "Just as well, isn't it?"

"Then who . . ."

"Just a messenger. That's all he was. Just a messenger."

They were swinging around again, and Golly recognized Columbus Circle ahead.

"Who killed him?" asked Golly, very quietly.

"Who do you think?" said Kahn.

"Why him?"

"Because they thought he was Control."

"You sure they weren't try to get me?"

"No, Michael," said the sandy-haired man from the back. "They weren't after you."

Golly got a chilly feeling. If they were right, if this had been planned for Control, and he was the one who had asked for a meeting with Control, and led him into it . . .

"That's right," said Kahn. "Doesn't exactly make you smell like a rose."

"How did they know about the meeting?" asked Golly.

"Ah," said the sandy-haired man.

They drove in silence. Kahn turned into Central Park.

"You don't think . . . that I . . ."

Golly knew he sounded like an accused man trying to clear himself in front of a stony-faced jury.

"It's not our job to think," said Kahn curtly. "It's our job to obey orders. Your job too."

"Switch on the radio," said the sandy-haired man. "It's news time."

Kahn turned a knob.

". . . the mystery shooting was in front of the capacity crowd at Madison Square Garden, but no one seems to have noticed the actual killing. The dead man has been identified as Tony Rosser, a jeweler, from Flatbush. Police are appealing for any witnesses to come forward, and a special appeal is being made for anyone who sat in the vicinity of the dead man . . ."

"I bet," said Kahn.

"A lead in the hunt is the spectator who sat next to Rosser, and hurriedly left in the middle of the performance. This man rushed out of the arena by a staff exit and hit Egon Padrewski, doyen of the twenty-five-strong Barnum clown troupe, who tried to question him. The mystery man is described as a Caucasian about thirty-five years old, five feet eleven inches, a hundred and forty pounds, gray eyes, dark hair, wearing a navy blazer and a brown and blue tie . . ."

"Christ," said Kahn, looking at Golly. Navy blazer, brown and blue tie. "Why didn't you leave a fucking calling card?"

Golly said nothing.

"Every cop in New York has that description now," snapped Kahn savagely.

"It's okay," said the sandy-haired man. "Lots of men wear navy blazers, are five feet eleven, and weigh a hundred and forty pounds. They're fishing, that's all."

"Glad you think so," said Kahn.

The announcer switched to Carter and a Congressional hearing about a new White House appointment.

"Turn it off," said the sandy-haired man. He seemed to be in charge.

"That's just great," glowered Kahn. "Every cop in New York . . ."

The glance he gave Golly was hate-filled.

"Forget that now," ordered the sandy-haired man. "Michael will watch himself. Won't you, Michael?"

But Golly's thoughts were elsewhere.

He was still thinking about the reason for meeting in the circus.

"What was the message?" asked Golly. "What was he supposed to tell me?"

"Your instructions," said Kahn. "From Central."

"What are they?"

"You are to return to London immediately. There you will be given your orders."

It was the sandy-haired man who said that.

Golly licked his lips.

"What about John Chance? What does Central say about him? Is he genuine?"

"That's all," said the sandy-haired man. "You'll be told everything you need to know in London."

"That *is* your territory," said Kahn, viciously. "Not New York."

"I *must* know about John Chance," said Golly.

"Well, you go back to London. Observe procedure. Central will know how to get hold of you," said the sandy-haired man.

"I must know more," said Golly.

"Maybe they don't want to tell you more," said Kahn. "Not after the way you've behaved."

"You trying to say I'm not trusted any more?"

"Not at all," said the sandy-haired man smoothly. "But it's really got nothing to do with us. It's a matter for the London station. The less *we* know the better for *us*."

Kahn said nothing.

"So how do I know if I can trust John Chance?"

"I'm sure it will all be made crystal clear to you," said the man. "Central was informed of your query and you will hear further. But in London. Keep away from us."

"I told you," muttered Kahn.

"You're booked on the nine o'clock flight in the morning," said the sandy-haired man. "It's all taken care of. British Airways. You must fly the flag, mustn't you?"

He allowed himself a thin smile.

"The sooner you get out of New York the better for everybody, Michael," he added.

They'd gone up through the park to Seventy-second Street and were now on Fifth Avenue.

"And in London I just wait?"

"Central has taken care of it," said the sandy-haired man, soothingly. "Leave it to them."

Kahn pulled up at the sidewalk outside a bookstore.

"You'd better get out here," he said, unfriendly.

"All right," said Golly, quietly.

Sandy hair leaned forward in the car.

"One thing, Michael. We don't exist, right? You don't know us. You've never seen us."

"You don't exist," said Golly, flatly.

He slammed the door, and the Chevrolet drove off at once.

Golly shivered. In his mind's eye, he kept seeing the red stain on the gray suit.

Moscow

46

Driving a staff Zim, with a government license plate, the major followed the circular highway from Moscow for some thirty kilometers, until the turn-off to Serebryany Bor came.

There he swung right and followed a road through the wood until he came to the privilege dachas, the official off-duty homes for those with special status.

The dachas stood by themselves, isolated from their neighbors, buried among the birch trees and the pines. Serebryany Bor means the "silver wood," and when frost settled on the trees, they glistened like candelabra.

But there were other things on the major's mind. To be summoned to the colonel's dacha did not bode well. It was no social occasion. He knew what the colonel had on the agenda. And he knew what it meant to discuss it in these unofficial surroundings.

The colonel took his unpleasant decisions here, away from the office, the corridors, the establishment. When he decided to stay away from headquarters for a day, and summoned one of the staff to his dacha instead, something was awkward.

There were people who had come away from the dacha relegated in rank, exiled to a dead-end assignment, briefed for a fatal mission, sometimes suspended —once, under open arrest.

The colonel was standing at the door of the dacha when the Zim pulled up. The major knew that among the trees there were electronic eyes and that this exclusive area, reserved for the hideaways of the prominent ones, was under close guard. He knew that anyone approaching it was under scrutiny and that probably his telltale MOC license plate was the reason he had not been checked.

But whether the colonel had received early warning that the Zim was getting near or whether it was just coincidence that he happened to be in the doorway, the major had no idea.

The colonel was not in a good temper, that was evident.

"I said nine a.m." he snapped as the major got out of the car.

"A truck jackknifed on the highway," apologized the major. "There was a traffic jam . . ."

"Hmm," grunted the colonel. "Come in."

The dacha was furnished like a hunting lodge, and that was what it served the colonel for. He actually had a villa fifty-one kilometers southeast of Moscow and a country home in the Crimea.

"Sit down," said the colonel. He did not offer the major any refreshments.

The major, who was in charge of Special Activities, waited, a little anxiously. He knew that all day yesterday the colonel had been in his office, going through the dossier.

"How could this happen?" asked the colonel, without warning.

The major shifted uneasily.

"Everything is now under control, comrade colonel," he said soothingly.

"Is it?"

The colonel seemed unimpressed.

"You've read the report from Zola?" he asked. Zola was the New York resident.

The major nodded.

"The situation should never have been allowed to arise," growled the colonel. "The procedures should be completely foolproof."

He took out a Dunhill cigarette, but didn't offer one

to the major. He was running low until his next consignment arrived in the diplomatic bag from the London embassy.

"Communication with deep-cover illegals has always had its special problems," said the major. "They must not know anything, or anyone, and this can lay them open . . ."

The colonel lit his cigarette.

"Tell me, Viktor Fedorovitch, is that what I am to say to the Directorate?" he asked, dangerously calm.

"What you can say is that we are immediately taking all the necessary steps," said the major. "It is all in my memorandum, in the file . . ."

The colonel regarded him with distaste.

"Reports, memoranda, notes, files, excuses. Our best network abroad running around chasing its own tail. One of our most carefully planted illegals not knowing whether he is coming or going. And you talk of papers and files."

"But at least we now know that Mikhail is completely loyal and trustworthy," said the major. "His conduct proves that."

"Did you have any doubts about him, then?" asked the colonel, very quietly.

"Of course not," said the major. He wished his collar wasn't so tight. The colonel wore comfortable civilian clothes, a woolen shirt, a leather hunting jacket. The major was in uniform. "But one is glad to be reassured. By the very nature of the beast, a long-term sleeper . . ."

"Do not refer to our dedicated operatives as beasts, Viktor Fedorovitch," said the colonel.

"But you know the risks with sleepers," persisted the major. "Isolated, out of touch, unable to communicate, lonely, subjected to the pressures of an alien society. That's what went wrong with Sabotka in Montreal, didn't it? And Lyalin in London. And Tuomi in Washington. All good men who cracked."

He picked out those names deliberately, with a touch of malice. The colonel had been their case officer. It served to remind him if he was trying to get heavy-handed now.

"Go on," said the colonel, watching him.

The major was suddenly conscious that the dacha was full of weapons. In the corner, a rack of hunting rifles, some with sniper telescopes. On one of the walls, a whole array of vicious-looking hunting knives.

"I am interested," said the colonel.

Uneasily, the major wondered if anyone had ever been killed in this dacha.

"Please pursue your theory," insisted the colonel.

There was a photograph on the wall, next to the balalaika hanging from a hook, of the colonel posing with a huge boar he had shot, the right foot triumphantly planted on the beast. The major licked his lips. He felt thirsty.

"Tuomi became so insecure, didn't he, that when he went to that football game between the New York Giants and the Washington Redskins he started weeping at the sight of the happy crowds, and began to talk . . ."

The major was warming to his theme.

"When a man is away from his homeland, he sometimes weakens, comrade colonel."

The colonel snorted.

"There will always be traitors, and we deal with them. But Mikhail is utterly reliable. And so are the others in his kind of operation. Like the man in the Sorbonne we have had there for twelve years, inactive. His local Control has changed four times without his ever knowing. The man in Melbourne has been on his own for nine years, just waiting for the call. As are the girl in Amsterdam and the Oslo man. Dedicated, all of them."

"Yes," said the major. When the colonel got in this mood, there was no point in arguing.

"They face great dangers of course," said the colonel. "Like Hentoff. Murdered in the line of duty. I think he deserves a decoration. Remind me."

"Of course, comrade colonel."

130

"Somebody got on to Hentoff," said the colonel. "And they killed him. Which makes me think Mikhail is in danger. After the business in New York, I am very worried."

"I agree," said the major. He wasn't a staff officer for nothing.

"If this whole thing turns into a debacle, all of us face corrective action," said the colonel. His voice underlined "corrective action" very slightly.

He put out his cigarette.

"The Illegal Organs Department is already sniffing around our section, and Sakharof would like nothing better than to have an excuse to swallow us."

Sakharof, a Georgian, had the same rank as the colonel, and both knew that only one of them would move upwards in the Directorate. Sakharof intended to make sure it wasn't the colonel, and the feeling was mutual.

The major, of course, had always seen to it that Sakharof got the best possible impression of him, and hoped he regarded him as a brilliant, dedicated intelligence officer who would be indispensable to any departmental head. Including Sakharof.

The colonel, whom little escaped, intended to make sure that the major fully realized that if the colonel fell from grace, so would the major.

"I'm sure nothing of the sort will happen," said the major.

"I hope not," said the colonel.

He had made a specialty of deploying deep-cover illegals in foreign countries.

And he knew his achievements were recognized by the General and, above him, the Director, and beyond.

But this new situation had to be resolved before it infected somebody else.

"We have worked too hard and too long to establish the London circle to let it be destroyed now," said the colonel. "It is your responsibility, Viktor Fedorovitch, that the whole Mikhail situation be stabilized. Your personal responsibility."

It was a warning as much as an order.

"Naturally," said the major.

The colonel stood up. The major also got to his feet.

"I will inform the Directorate that the necessary action is being taken, and that the London situation is about to be dealt with," said the colonel, rather officially, as if speaking for the record.

"Yes, comrade colonel," said the major, equally officially.

Suddenly the colonel became full of bonhomie.

"You are quite clear what has to be done?" he asked the major, putting his arm around his shoulders and steering him toward the door.

"Of course."

"It's a pity in many ways. The craft of intelligence is a delicate art. It has great elegance. Killing people belongs to another sphere. It is more Sakharof's style."

"Nevertheless, there are times when it has to be done," said the major.

They stopped at the door.

"Unfortunately, you are right, Viktor Fedorovitch," agreed the colonel. "And I regret that this is one such time. He will have to be disposed of."

He walked the major to the parked Zim.

"I will be at headquarters tomorrow," he said.

"I look forward to that, comrade colonel," said the major.

As he drove back through the wood, he wondered if it was true that the colonel was having an affair with Antonova, the ballerina. And if, on the odd night away from the office, he brought her to this remote dacha.

Somehow, the major didn't think that a woman as sensitive and artistic as Antonova would particularly appreciate the guns and the knives and the photo of the dead boar.

In the dacha, the colonel lit another Dunhill. He had only four left now.

He paced up and down. The colonel felt restless.

He was worried about the London business. He hoped it would work out. He hoped that no mistakes would be made.

He walked over to the rack, and took down a hunting rifle. From a drawer, he took some cartridges and loaded the magazine.

Then he went out of the dacha, cradling the gun. He strolled along a path and then branched off among the trees.

Once he heard a rustle in the undergrowth, but there was nothing to see. Nothing to hunt.

He felt frustrated. The Mikhail business was giving him more anxiety than he had bargained for.

On the way back to the dacha, he spotted a squirrel on the branch of a tree.

He raised his rifle, fired, and blew the squirrel's head off.

It made him feel a bit better.

London

47

Golly cleared customs and carried his bag over to the taxi stand. There were seven or eight people ahead of him, including a Pakistani with five huge trunks and four enormous paper-wrapped bundles.

The cabs appeared, one by one, and picked up the next in line. Golly reckoned it would take at least ten minutes before his turn came.

"How was New York?"

Golly swung around.

John Chance was standing at his side, smiling.

For a moment, Golly didn't know what to say.

"Here, let me take that," said Chance, and grabbed Golly's suitcase. "The car's around the corner."

He led the way and Golly walked by his side, trying to think quickly. He felt as if he were being led like a captive animal.

"I didn't expect to see you here," said Golly.

"Of course not," said Chance. "But it's so depressing to get back on one's own and find nobody's bothered to show up."

"Nobody knew I'd be on this flight," said Golly.

Chance smiled. "I did," he said.

They came to the mini, and Chance put the bag in the back.

"How did *you* know?"

Chance still smiled. "How do you think?" he asked. "Get in, Mike."

He started the car, and swung around out of the car park, toward the underpass.

"Good to have you back," he said, and he sounded very sincere.

They said nothing in the airport tunnel, but at the roundabout, on the main road, Chance, looking straight in front, suddenly said, "Well?"

"The flight wasn't bad," said Golly. "There was an awful Walt Disney film, but I slept through most of it."

He knew that wasn't what John Chance wanted to know.

"Mike."

"Yes?" said Golly.

"You've been very naughty again. You realize that? Everybody is annoyed."

"Who is?" asked Golly, all innocent.

Chance ignored him.

"Personally, I don't blame you at all," he went on. "In your position, I would have done the same. One needs to be reassured, doesn't one?"

"How is Sharon?" asked Golly, as if he hadn't heard Chance.

"Sharon?" For a moment, Chance seemed taken aback.

"Have you seen anything of her?"

It sounded almost disinterested.

Chance had quite recovered his composure.

"Wish I had," he said. "We must all get together, now you're home."

Smoothly, he added, "Have you heard from her?"

"I thought she might have given you a call," said Golly. He was determined not to let go. "Asked you over for a game of chess, or something."

"Chess?"

Chance looked startled.

"Didn't you know?" said Golly. "Sharon is a very good chess player."

"I'm sure Sharon has many talents," said Chance.

They drove on in silence, past the Hogarth roundabout, into Chiswick, toward Hammersmith Town Hall.

"What happens now?" asked Golly.

"We carry on," said Chance. He gave Golly a sidelong glance. "Now that you are fully satisfied."

Golly said nothing.

"You are, aren't you?"

For once, there was a touch of anxiety in Chance's tone.

Golly shrugged, "Maybe. They said I would hear further. Direct. In London."

Chance nodded. "Exactly. And you have. That's why I met you."

Golly stared at him.

"Oh, for heaven's sake," said Chance wearily. "What do you want? Blood group and fingerprints? You got them to check with Central, right? And I got instructions to meet you and tell you all about it. Because that's the proof, Mike. That I know. That I have been told."

Golly waited for more.

"Yes," said Chance. "I've been told. Everything. Even that there was trouble in New York. That somebody took a pot shot. That's the reason I warned you, Mike. Remember? It's all got very dangerous."

"I know," said Golly, very quietly.

"I think they may be out to kill you," said Chance. "I know they're after me."

He said it very calmly.

"Who?" asked Golly.

That annoyed Chance. "Don't be naïve. It's a new technique. People like us are hard to replace, so the other side likes to put us out of circulation. We are a valuable commodity."

"But who is it?" pressed Golly.

"You mean, who is the man? What does he look like? I wish I knew. For all our sakes."

"No idea?" asked Golly. "None at all?"

Chance shook his head as they slid into the traffic

toward Shepherd's Bush, past the Palais and the police station.

"I know he got Hentoff," said Chance, savagely. "Maybe he was the one who got Rosser."

"Rosser?"

"Your contact. In New York. Maybe our man was with you over there, the whole time."

"And he'll be back here now?"

"Of course," said Chance. "That's why we'll all have to be very careful."

They got to Holland Park and, near Golly's flat, Chance pulled up to the curb. Golly remembered the time Chance had stopped here and dropped her.

"Will this do you?"

"Come up to the house," said Golly.

"No, thanks," said Chance. "Not this time. I'm sure Sharon wants you to herself."

"Just for a cup . . ."

"Very kind, but not now," said Chance.

He looked at Golly reflectively. Then he pulled an envelope out of his pocket.

"Here," he said. He held it out to Golly. "Take it."

"What's this?"

"Go on, open it."

Golly tore open the flap. Inside was a snapshot.

A picture of a pretty girl. Dark, curly-haired, smiling. In a white blouse.

Golly stared at it, frozen.

"Recognize her?" said Chance, softly.

For a moment the world had stopped. It was the past overtaking the present. It was something that had been shut away, because that's the way it had to be.

"Where did you get this?" gasped Golly.

"Doesn't she look well?" said Chance. "She's a real credit to you."

"Please," said Golly. "Please. Tell me."

"It was taken last Tuesday. I'm sure you'll recognize the background. It came over by, shall we say, diplomatic means."

140

Golly looked at the picture of his daughter, standing in Red Square, and for a moment all else was forgotten.

"She's doing very well at the university," said Chance.

Golly was staring at the photograph as if the girl would step out of it.

"Her mother must have been a very attractive woman, Mikhail," said Chance.

It was the first time ever he had used the Russian version.

And it brought Golly back into the present.

"Does she know . . . ?"

Chance shook his head. "Nothing. She doesn't and she mustn't. She's well looked after, and happy. And she's a lovely girl. You're very lucky."

"Am I?" said Golly, and he sounded sad.

"I know," said John Chance, and he was very gentle. "It isn't easy. It isn't easy for any of us. Sometimes I . . ."

He stopped.

Golly put the photo back in the envelope and placed it in his breast pocket.

"Thank you," he said simply. "You don't know what that picture means to me."

"Maybe I do," said Chance. "Maybe it does something else."

"Yes," said Golly. "That picture comes from Central."

"Exactly," said Chance. "It was taken by Viktor Fedorovitch."

He helped Golly get the suitcase out of the back of the mini.

"You sure you won't come in for a minute?" asked Golly.

"Some other time," said Chance. "Be seeing you."

And the mini shot off into the night.

48

"Mike," she said, and they held each other close, and he knew he was home.

She felt wonderful, near to him, and with her there, everything suddenly seemed much more secure.

"Thank God you're back," she said.

She said it fervently.

"Anything wrong?" he asked, disengaging himself gently.

"Not that way," she said.

"What do you mean?"

"It doesn't feel right without you."

"Silly idiot," he said, but he loved hearing her make the remark. He wanted to be missed. He needed to be needed.

She loved the bracelet he had bought her.

"You've got good taste," she said, holding out her arm at length and admiring the circlet on her wrist.

He was very tired. Some New Yorkers were still having breakfast when he left, and now, here in London, it was close on midnight, although he had not been flying much more than six hours.

The intermittent naps in the plane, the plastic meals, the shirt sticking to him, the corridors and barriers, the monotony had all dulled his senses.

And the shock of what John Chance had shown him was only now hitting him, like a cavity that only starts hurting when the numbness wears off.

"What was New York like?" she asked.

Stupidly, his mind registered the fact that it was the second time that evening somebody had asked him the same question.

"Tiring," he said.

"Did you see any good shows?"

"I went to the circus," said Golly.

"The circus! What on earth for?"

"I like the circus," said Golly. "Somebody gave me a ticket."

"What a funny thing to do," she said. "I wouldn't go to a circus in New York."

"Why not?"

"Well, that's the sort of thing you can do here. We've got circuses."

"Not one like that," said Golly.

"Did you like it, after all that?"

"It was interesting."

Later, in the dark, she reached for his hand.

"Mike."

"Yes?"

"Did—did you see Ellen?"

He thought, Oh, not that.

"No."

"Didn't you try?"

"No."

She was silent.

"So there's nothing new," she said at last.

"No. Nothing new."

She sighed. "Never mind."

He reached for her, and she responded.

He felt her merge with him and then, in his mind's eye, he was in bed with another Sharon. He suddenly had a vivid memory of her, dark-haired, enigmatic, her lips invitingly apart, her smell, her taut body. And he resented the way she had momentarily forced her way into their privacy. It was almost, in the darkness, like a second woman in bed with him.

"You're hurting," said Sharon, in a small voice. It wasn't a complaint, just a plea: Do what gives you pleasure, but don't be so rough.

He kissed her, hard, holding her, feeling her, but the other Sharon still loomed, mocking him.

Afterwards, she said gently, "Mike, I'm glad you're home."

But he was already asleep, and he never heard her say it.

49

"You think this is true?" asked Sir Deryck. He looked across at Foxglove hopefully, waiting to hear reassuring words.

"I'm afraid it is," said Foxglove.

"Are you sure?" asked Sir Deryck, and blinked. He often blinked when an unpalatable situation confronted him.

"I am," said Foxglove.

"Oh," said Sir Deryck.

"It'll be interesting to see the course things now take," said Foxglove. "I find it quite intriguing."

"It's messy," said Sir Deryck. "The whole business is messy."

The note of reproach was quite clear: You should not allow this kind of thing to come along to bother us.

Foxglove reflected, not for the first time, that Sir Deryck should really have headed the department—if it had existed—under Palmerston. He didn't exactly share Stimson's opinion that gentlemen don't read other gentlemen's mail, and he didn't mind Ruritanian intrigue, but the hard, nasty, vicious side of the business he would much rather not know about.

And, if Foxglove had his way, he usually wouldn't anyway.

Unfortunately, certain reports and files were marked "Attn: DD," and Sir Deryck was DD. Reports like the one lying on his clean desk now.

"We should always avoid bloodshed," said Sir Deryck. He was the one who had insisted that Blake be flown back from Beirut instead of having a fatal accident in a back alley in that salubrious city. He had allowed Philby to take up the newspaper job after others had suggested there might be more drastic ways of dealing with the gentleman. And departmental rumor had it that Burgess and Maclean were only able to slip out of the trap because it happened to be a weekend, and Sir Deryck did not believe in business on a weekend. So the warrant had to wait till Monday.

"I am biased against it," said Foxglove, carefully. "It can boomerang."

"Indeed," said Sir Deryck. "I am sorry the Director is on leave at the moment. Otherwise I would ask him to intervene."

"In his absence, you are perfectly entitled, Sir Deryck . . ."

Foxglove did not finish the sentence. What he meant was, You have authority to do all the intervening you want.

Sir Deryck blinked.

"I do not believe in interfering in operational matters in the field," he said primly.

What he meant, of course, was, I will not stick my neck out and have to take final responsibility in something as delicate as this. Foxglove knew that was what he meant, and he knew that Foxglove knew it.

"Very well then, Gerald," said Sir Deryck. "I only wanted to reassure myself that this report is factual and that the situation is indeed what it says."

"I believe all the departmental reports that pass through my section are factual," sniffed Foxglove haughtily. They all were, too, except the blind ones, which had no carbon copies and weren't typed by secretaries.

"Of course, Gerald," said Sir Deryck genially. "Absolutely. But there have been times, in my years in the service, when I have read absolute fiction. Sheer spy fiction."

He laughed at his own wit.

"I wish this one was," said Foxglove, without a smile. "It would make life rather easier."

"And perhaps a little less dangerous?"

Foxglove shot a quick look at Sir Deryck.

For once, the eyes were not blinking.

50

When Golly opened his eyes, Sharon was already up. He looked at the bedside clock. It was 11:15.

"Christ," said Golly.

He put on a dressing gown, stepped into his slippers, and went into the kitchen.

"Do you know what the time is?" he asked Sharon. "You should have woken me."

"You want some coffee?" she asked coldly.

Her tone was flat.

"Yes, please," he said. "My first English coffee. That'll be a change."

She said nothing. She did not smile. She did not react. She just put the coffee in front of him.

"Thanks," said Golly, giving her a curious look. "Did you sleep well?"

"Quite well, thank you," she said, stiffly.

Something was wrong, all right.

"What's the matter?" he asked.

"What should be the matter?" said Sharon, blankly. No warmth. No rapport.

"Come and sit down," said Golly.

"I'm busy," said Sharon, bustling.

"I want to talk to you," he said.

"I have things to do," she retorted, unyielding.

He found himself getting angry.

"They can wait," he said.

She turned around to face him.

"I'm taking your suit to the cleaners," she said.

He didn't get it.

"The suit you wore in New York," she said pointedly.

What the hell was going on?

"Yes," he said. "It's creased to hell. All that sitting about in the plane.

She looked at him accusingly. Waiting.

"What's this all about, Sharon?" he asked.

She opened a kitchen drawer, took out an envelope.

"This," she said, holding out the envelope. "This is what it's all about."

He took it, but he didn't have to look inside.

It was the snapshot. He knew.

"I had to go through your pockets to get the suit ready," she said. "I found this."

"Yes," he said, dully.

"Well?"

"What about it?" he demanded.

How the devil could he explain?

"Who is she, Michael?"

"A girl," he said.

"Don't get clever," she snapped. "Who is she?"

Desperately, he tried to work out a story. Any story.

"It's not what you think . . ." he said lamely.

"Why, what do I think?" she challenged.

"She's just a young girl," he said. "She's only seventeen. Only just turned seventeen."

She raised her eyebrows.

"Bit young for you, isn't she?"

"I just can't explain," he said, and he knew how stupidly inadequate that sounded.

"I think you'd better," said Sharon.

She went over and poured herself some coffee.

"Look, Michael, I'm not trying to be a jealous bitch," she said. "I know it sounds like it. But really, I'm not. I just sometimes feel so—desperately insecure. There's that wife of yours. In New York. You've only just been there. You rushed over mysteriously. I don't even know why. You come back. You're carrying a photo of this girl. She's very pretty. I don't know who she is. I don't even know where I am any more . . ."

She was crying.

He got up and put his arm around her as he always did.

"You are here, love," he said gently. "With me. We're together. Just us. Nobody else."

She looked up at him, tears smudging her face.

"Who is she?" she almost begged. "Tell me. Michael, please."

Her eyes were pleading.

He knew he mustn't do it.

"She's not what you think at all," he said. "She's not a girl friend. Never has been. It's nothing like that."

"Is she your daughter, Michael?" asked Sharon, very quietly.

Oh God, he thought.

"What—what makes you think that?" he whispered.

"Well, if she's not . . . and she looks like you a bit, doesn't she?"

What do I do? he kept asking himself, and no reply came.

"That's it, isn't it? She *is* your daughter?"

"Yes," he said.

She took the envelope and looked at the snapshot.

"She's nice," said Sharon. "What's her name?"

"Mary," he lied. Don't tell the real name. It would betray too much, reveal too much

Sharon looked more closely at the picture.

"Where was this taken?" she asked.

"On the continent," he said. Christ, once you open the can of beans . . .

"They're spires, sort of, aren't they?" said Sharon, peering at the photograph intently. "And that wall—Do you know something? It's the Kremlin. I think it's Red Square. In Moscow."

She looked at Michael triumphantly.

"What's your daughter doing in Moscow?" she asked.

"Oh, some sort of trip," he said vaguely.

She put the picture down.

"Why did you never tell me you had a daughter?" she asked

"I don't know," he said. He knew very well why. "It's a bit complicated."

"Does she live with your—wife?"

"No," he said.

"She's on her own?" asked Sharon, surprised. "Where? New York?"

"I haven't seen her for a long time," said Golly. "Not for years."

"Why on earth not? You're her father, aren't you?"

"She's all right," he said, defensively. "She's fine."

"You ought to invite her over," said Sharon. "I'd love to meet her."

"She's so busy studying . . ." he said "One day, perhaps . . ."

"Do you ever hear from her?" Sharon asked.

"I just have," he said. "A friend . . ."

"That's how you got the photo?"

He nodded.

"Oh, Michael," said Sharon, "I do feel a cow. I'm a real louse."

"You sound like the zoo," he said. "Why on earth do you—"

"I'm really ashamed of myself. Giving you the hurt little woman act. You have every right to kick me."

"I only want to kiss you," he said, and embraced her. His heart felt much lighter. Just mentioning it to Sharon, mentioning some of it, lifted part of the dreadful load. At least she shared one little piece of the jigsaw now. It was only a half-truth, but it was at last some of the truth.

Only later, when he realized that for the first time in seven years he had come near to revealing some of the truth about part of himself, did he wonder if he had not made a mistake.

A fatal mistake.

51

He didn't have a gun, and now he began to wonder seriously if he shouldn't somehow acquire one.

Michael Golly led a scrupulously legal existence. He paid his television license the moment he got the reminder, he always told the bus conductor his destination and did not ride one stop beyond, and his income tax was a model of copybook returns and punctual payments.

That was the price of being completely illegal.

He didn't run a car, and one reason was that, in modern life, it would inevitably bring him into minor conflict with the law. Driving and its possible consequences could lead to other complications.

And he had no gun.

Possessing one unlawfully would be far too great a risk. If he carried it, and somebody spotted it, he'd be finished. If he kept it in a drawer and the house was burgled and the gun taken, he could be in terrible trouble. They'd find out for sure.

And what did he need one for anyway?

His mission would never be assassination. Violence was outside his type of operation. If that was needed, they would send an expert. Illegals like himself weren't planted and secreted away for some crude physical action. They worked in a much more subtle, sophisticated kind of field.

And, of course, while they had kept him asleep, he had been perfectly safe. Nobody knew about him, or cared a damn. Nobody was interested in him. That was the essence of it. Be insignificant, and nobody notices you. Stay out of any kind of hassle, and nobody will be aware of you. Friend or foe.

But the fear that had been gnawing at him was now slowly becoming part of his daily life. He had seen a man die next to him. Die ridiculously, among laughing, clapping people, with clowns cavorting and acrobats balancing. But die very suddenly, and effectively. Just as the man Hentoff appeared to have died.

And just as he himself might die if he wasn't careful, John Chance had hinted.

So, for the first time, he wished that he had a gun. He wasn't quite sure how it would help him. The killer, if he came, probably wouldn't advertise himself. He doubted if Hentoff had seen the man who

pushed him. He knew that the contact in New York
—what was his name? Rosser?—had never known that
a silenced gun was aiming at him in that crowd.

Golly realized that, if he were the next target, a
gun would probably be of little assistance He would
possibly not even have a chance to use it. But at least
it would give him a great feeling of security and the
satisfaction, possibly, of at least being able to take
one single shot at his killer as he lay dying.

Dying. What the hell was the matter with him,
accepting that almost as a likely event? He was
damned if he was going to die. They'd find out, whoever they were, that he was no clay pigeon.

But a gun? Was it worth all the problems it cre-
ated? Already the cloak of complete secure secrecy
with which he had so carefully been wrapped was
becoming threadbare; Sharon knew about his daughter, he had contacted Kahn and his section. Bit by
bit the mystery on which he relied to protect himself
was being stripped away.

Of course, he could get hold of a gun. In a Soho
bar, an East End cafè, a wad of ten-pound notes
would buy anything, no questions asked.

Then what?

No, he decided. Watch yourself. Don't make stupid
mistakes. Take great care. Watch every word you say.
Don't get involved in anything. Stay out of trouble.
Live like a cabbage, until they summon you.

But no gun.

52

Two days later, Sharon said:

"Mr. Richardson phoned."

"Who?"

"Don't you know him?" she said. "He seemed to
know you."

Golly's stomach tightened.

"What did he say?"

"He'd call back. Tonight. At eight."

"Oh, all right," he said, trying to sound disinterested.

"Who is he?" said Sharon, very offhand.

"No idea."

"Funny," she said. "He sounded just as if he knew you"

53

"Full surveillance?" repeated Baron, and his dismay was obvious.

"Full surveillance," said Foxglove.

"The whole time?"

"Twenty-four hours," nodded Foxglove.

"But, sir . . ."

"Yes?" said Foxglove, and stopped beside the green Volkswagen. It was parked next to a Buick with Florida license plates, and two Fiats, both with "Visitor to Britain" labels stuck on their windscreens. The Radio Rentals van was in its bay, and near it a furniture-removal truck, two station wagons, and a row of Cortinas, Vauxhalls, and three Datsuns. There were also Volvos and a Skoda, and a couple of Hillman Minxes. These actually looked official.

They were in the department's garage in Battersea, which housed the operational motor pool. It had a small radio room on the first floor, but outwardly it looked like a not too successful hire-car business. The odd stranger who now and then actually wandered in wanting to hire a car was told they were all bespoken. What he didn't know was that while he stood there, he was also filmed. Just in case he turned out to have other interests besides hiring a weekend car.

"Twenty-four-hour surveillance needs a team," said Baron. "Eight men, minimum. We always used to do it that way, and we found that was the least number."

"No more," said Foxglove. "We've had to cut costs."

"How many cars?" asked Baron.

Foxglove indicated the vehicles around them.

"Take your pick," he said, grandly.

"It means three cars on the trot any one time," said Baron. "It's essential for relay shadowing."

"One car," said Foxglove firmly.

"One car for a twenty-four-hour surveillance?"

Baron was living up to his image, thought Foxglove. Repeating all the unpalatable things, as if he were talking to an idiot.

"One car is all we can spare," said Foxglove "Transport budget has been cut thirty-one per cent."

"How can they, sir?" asked Baron. "We're essential."

"Glad you think so," said Foxglove. "They seem to have their doubts."

"London area, this job?" asked Baron.

"Mostly, I imagine," said Foxglove vaguely.

"And it's down to me?"

"You're very experienced," said Foxglove. Yes, he thought, you are, too. The last subject you were following was murdered in front of your eyes.

"Thank you, sir," said Baron, and almost stiffened, like a soldier picked to save a besieged garrison. He might not make it, but the Victoria Cross was a certainty.

"Good," said Foxglove. "We'd better get back to town, then."

Anything more than two miles was out of town for Foxglove. Anything south of the Thames was foreign parts. It was one reason he loathed going to the National Theatre.

Baron thought Foxglove would pick one of the cars in the garage, but Foxglove walked down Lavender Hill with him, looking for a cab.

"Who is the subject?" asked Baron.

"For this job?"

Baron nodded expectantly.

153

"A rather dangerous man," said Foxglove.

"Oh, yes?"

"Unfortunately, we don't know yet who he is."

Baron gaped.

"But—but how do we watch a man we don't know?"

Foxglove waved at an empty taxi.

"That does make it a little difficult, doesn't it?" he said, beaming.

54

One minute past eight, the phone rang in Golly's flat. Sharon was watching television and took no notice as he rushed into the hall.

He picked up the phone and gave his number.

He could hear the pip-pip-pip of a call box at the other end, and then the clunk of the coin dropping.

"Michael?" said a man's voice. It was soft, gentle.

"Yes," said Golly. His heart was pounding.

"This is Ian Richardson," said the voice.

"Yes," said Golly.

"We have a mutual friend," said the voice.

"Who?" asked Golly.

"There is a call box in Page Street. At the corner with Regency Street. Westminster. Perhaps you could be there at nine o'clock. *Ciao*."

The phone clicked. Whoever it was had put the receiver down.

Golly's hand was shaking slightly

He went into the living room.

"I've got to go out for a bit," he told Sharon.

"Was that Mr. Richardson?" she asked, without taking her eyes off the television screen. She seemed engrossed in a miserably boring play about a mental cripple in braces having incest with his mongoloid daughter.

"Yes," he said.

"Are you meeting him for a drink or something?" she asked.

"Yes," he said.

She turned around and gave him a smile.

"All right. I don't know how long I can stand this, so I may push off."

"I won't be late," he said.

"Have a good time," she said.

"It's business," he muttered, and then wished he hadn't.

When he left the house, he looked up and down, but there didn't seem to be anyone around.

On Holland Park Avenue, he hailed a cab.

55

As soon as he paid off the cab, he realized why the man who called himself Ian Richardson had picked this particular phone booth, at this particular spot.

It was absolutely deserted. The whole neighborhood was empty. Somewhere was a pub, and he could hear the sounds of singing. Once, a car came down the street, but it stood out like a lone ship in the night and, because there was absolutely no traffic, it raced past at high speed.

Otherwise there was no sign of life.

The phone box stood empty, its light on.

Golly looked at his watch. The cab had taken the route via Vauxhall Bridge Road, and the journey went faster than he had expected. There was still twenty minutes before nine.

Golly followed the noise of the singing and came to the pub. Inside, it was surprisingly crowded. Here were the people who lived in these huge blocks of silent council flats that lined the street. And in here, they were not silent.

He pushed his way through the noisy crowd to the bar and asked for a Scotch. When he asked for ice, one cube was grudgingly put in his glass.

He leaned back against the bar and stared around. Was he here? Was he, too, killing time before they met up at that silent streetcorner, by the phone kiosk?

Was he that fat man with the drooping eyelids? Or that curious creature in sandals, with uncut hair tumbling down to his shoulders? Was he that prim little character drinking by himself in a striped suit and a regimental tie? Or that man in shirtsleeves, demolishing a meat pie in half a dozen greedy mouthfuls?

And which pair of eyes was examining him? wondered Golly. Had he been noticed as he entered, observed as he stared around curiously, analyzed as he sipped his whisky?

Was there somebody, something he had missed?

A man was banging away at a piano, and then some people began singing, and a tune Golly had always liked, a cheerful, joyous tune, was raucously raped and the noise, gradually, became insufferable.

He looked at his watch again. Six minutes to go. He drank up, put the glass down on the counter, and pushed his way out.

In the street, it was again eerily silent. Only the singing drifted out of the pub, but there wasn't anybody about, as far as his eye could see.

And nobody followed him out of the pub either.

Golly walked back to the corner and the phone booth. Two minutes to nine.

There wasn't a soul around. Not even a car coming down either of the streets.

He frowned. In the cab he had wondered momentarily if he was walking into some kind of ambush. But that seemed nonsensical, really. Part of his neurosis. He was sure that this was no setup. At least, he thought he was sure . . .

Nervously, he paced around, just a few steps one way, a few steps back again.

He was quite surprised when the woman appeared. She was elephantine. Her hair was in curlers, and she had slippers on her feet. Her ankles were swollen, and her face was greasy. She suddenly waddled up to the phone booth, and Golly had never noticed her approaching.

"You using this?" she asked belligerently.

"No," said Golly.

Without a word, she went into the phone booth She had a crumpled piece of paper and she spread it out on the little shelf, and then, painstakingly, she dialed a number and put the coin in.

Where was he, damn it?

Golly didn't want to make her think he was even remotely interested in her call. He moved off, looking up and down. It was now after nine.

He became conscious suddenly of the fact that although these empty streets were a backwater, they were extremely well lit. One could see a good distance. There were few shadows, no dark corners.

One could see well . . . and be seen.

He glanced at the woman. Now he saw for the first time that she had a handful of coins. She was just feeding another one into the box. She was obviously having a great chat He could see a trickle of sweat on her fat neck. He wondered why on earth she wore the curlers at nine o'clock in the evening. Did she take them off when she went to bed? Or did she want to look smart at breakfast? Or did she think curlers were the end in themselves, the sign of a woman of fashion? Sharon would die, he knew, rather than be seen in things like curlers.

Seven minutes after nine.

A white sports car appeared in the distance, and he saw it come toward the road junction. As it got nearer, he could see the driver. A girl. The car raced past, the girl's long blonde hair streaming.

But it never stopped.

And there was no one about in the street. Not along Page Street. Not down Regency Street.

In the phone kiosk, the woman slammed down the receiver. She came out of the booth, gave Golly another belligerent look.

"Ta," she said, surprisingly, considering her aggressive expression.

Then she waddled off.

He wondered how long he should stay here. Maybe something was wrong. Maybe Richardson . . .

Whoever he was. Whatever he might want. The back of Golly's neck prickled as he thought of that gentle, soft voice. Maybe he should contact John Chance. If he knew how . . .

Suddenly, the phone rang. Inside the call box.

Golly stared through the glass panes at the phone receiver. Then he realized.

He rushed into the booth, picked up the receiver. He could hear the pip-pip-pip again, the coin drop.

"Michael," said the voice. "I am sorry. I couldn't get through. The line was busy."

"Some woman was using it," said Golly.

"What a nuisance. Never mind."

Golly was thinking, Christ, he *is* careful. He arranges to call me at a box in a deserted street, and rings up from another public call box somewhere else. Public phone to public phone. No private number that can be traced. No line that is monitored.

"Where are you?" asked Golly.

There was a soft laugh.

"In London, old boy. I think we ought to meet, don't you?"

"Who is our mutual friend?" asked Golly. It was safe. Nobody could listen in on this.

"One of them has a delicatessen in New York," said the gentle voice. "Avenue of the Americas. Sixth Avenue, if you prefer. That's one of 'em."

"I see," said Golly. That's what he had known all along, really.

"Are you free tomorrow?" asked the voice, diffidently.

"Yes," said Golly.

"Oh, good," said the man called Ian Richardson. "Let's meet in the morning, about eleven. Platform three Edgware Road Station. You know, the Metro-

politan line. The last carriage but one on the first
Putney train that leaves after eleven. You got that?"

"Yes," said Golly. "First Putney train after eleven.
Last carriage but one."

"Fine," said the voice. "I look forward to that."

"How will I know you?" asked Golly.

He could hear the smile in the man's voice as he
answered.

"Don't worry about it, Mikhail," he said. "I'll know
you."

And he hung up.

56

"Did you have a nice time?" asked Sharon when he
got in just before midnight. She was already in bed.

"I told you, it was business," he said, irritably. He
had been doing a lot of thinking.

"Well, I hope it was nice business," she said.

When he came in from the bathroom, she put
down the magazine she had been reading.

"What's he like?" she asked.

"All right," he said. "What's he supposed to be
like?"

"I only asked, love," she said gently. "Don't snap
my head off."

"I'm sorry. I've had a lot on my mind."

"You're tired, Mike," she said soothingly. "Come
to bed."

He sat on the edge of the bed and started taking
his shoes off.

"How would you like to live abroad?" he suddenly
aske.

"Leave England, you mean?"

"Yes," he said.

"Where?" she asked, very quietly.

"I don't know," he said. "Abroad, away from things.
Mexico, maybe. Switzerland. I don't know."

"America."

He frowned. "I don't know," he repeated. "Maybe."

She laughed.

"Or how about Russia?"

He swung around, staring at her.

"Why Russia?" he asked, tersely.

She shrugged her naked shoulders. When the mood took her, she wore nothing in bed.

"Why not?" she said. "At least it would be different, if that's what you're after. I couldn't stand Australia, or New Zealand. Beer-drinking and sheep. Ugh."

"No, I'm serious," he said. "Just a little place somewhere. In the country. Where nobody knows anybody, or cares."

"Mike," she said.

"Hmm."

"Why do you want to go abroad?"

"Don't you just feel sometimes this place has had it?" he said, as if that were the real reason. "What future is there over here? Look what's been happening. They're so bloody stupid."

"They?"

"The English," he snapped.

"I like England," said Sharon very gently.

"So do I," he said, "but there comes a time . . ."

"Well, we don't have to make up our mind now, do we?" said Sharon, like a schoolmistress cutting off a stupid child in a pointless discussion.

"I don't know," he said.

She sat up in bed. She did not cover her breasts with the sheet. She was not shy with him.

"You really want to leave here?" she asked, worried.

"I only want to know how you'd feel about it," he said, "if it happened . . ."

"Mike, you can't expect me to answer just like that. Don't you understand? My mother is here. My friends. I have grown up here. This is my home."

"Yes," he said sadly.

"I mean, if you *had* to go, if you were in some sort

of trouble . . ." She stopped. "Mike," she said anxiously, "you're not in trouble, are you? That's not what it's all about? You must tell me, if it is."

"No," he said. He laughed. "It's not as dramatic as that." He hoped it sounded convincing. "It's just the way things are. Too much tax. Too much bad news. Too much bloody nothing. Too much boredom."

Her eyes flickered.

"You're not bored with me, are you?"

He came over to her and took her in his arms and convinced her.

After they had settled down, she said sleepily, "Mike."

"Go to sleep."

"No, Mike, I want to know. It's not that man Richardson, is it?"

He was suddenly very much awake again.

"Why should it be? Don't be silly."

She snuggled down.

"Good," she said, and she sounded relieved. "I just wondered suddenly, when you started talking like that, whether it had something to do with Richardson. Bad news or something. I only wondered."

"You're very sweet," he said, and he meant it.

But it was the Putney train and a fat woman in curlers and a gun with a silencer and a grinning clown and a Westminster school tie and a man screaming as he died that were all mixed up in the nightmare he had after he fell asleep.

57

The last carriage but one was empty when Golly sat down in it. The train had few passengers at that time in the morning, at least when it started out from Edgware Road.

Then the man arrived.

He was somehow younger than Golly had expected.

His features were finely chiseled, haughty, almost aristocratic. It was a strangely medieval face that would have fit into the court of the Borgias or a council of war of the Medici or on a tribunal of the Inquisition much better than on the Metropolitan line.

He entered the carriage, looked around as if to select a place to sit, and then, almost as though by accident, spotted Golly.

His face lit up.

"Michael," he said, delightedly, coming over and holding out his hand. "Fancy meeting you here."

He sat down beside Golly, who glanced quickly through the window. Nobody on the platform seemed to be paying the slightest attention to their carriage or to them.

"How far are you going?" asked Richardson.

"Putney, I think," said Golly.

"I've got the same ticket, then." Richardson smiled. He sat back and took in Golly's whole appearance.

"I've been looking forward to this," he said.

They could've been old friends who hadn't come across each other for far too long.

"The only Ian Richardson I've heard of is an actor," said Golly. "At the Royal Shakespeare."

"Well, I'm not he," said Richardson. "What a funny thought."

He looked out of the window.

"The train should start soon," he said.

He took out a packet of Dunhill cigarettes.

"Smoke?" he asked.

Golly took one, and Richardson lit both cigarettes.

"The colonel smokes these now," he said. "He got bored with the American ones."

"How is the colonel?" asked Golly.

The doors of the train slid shut.

"A little put out about things," said Richardson. "But not with you."

The electric motor started humming, and the train began to move westwards.

"Something seems to have gone badly wrong, Michael."

"Really?" said Golly.

"Central has sent me," said Richardson, quite matter-of-fact. "New York passed over your problem, and I'm here to sort it out."

"I see," said Golly.

"I have something for you," said Richardson. "By way of credentials, so to speak."

He brought out a handsome crocodile-skin wallet, much more expensive than his style of clothes. Out of it he took three photos.

"The colonel thought you'd like to see your daughter," he said.

The train had pulled into Paddington and started off again, but Golly was still clutching the three photos.

It was she, all right. In the same white blouse. Looking the same. But the background was different.

"Where was this taken?" asked Golly.

"Let's see," said Richardson, taking the photos. "Ah, yes. This one's outside the puppet theater, isn't it? In Mayakovsky Square. Oh, here she's on Gorky Street. And that's the Moskva Hotel, I think. Yes. It is."

He handed them back to Golly.

"Who took them?" asked Golly.

"Viktor Fedorovitch," said Richardson, nodding, as if approving Golly's question. "You remember the major?"

Golly stared at the photos.

"He took her to lunch at the Peking," said Richardson. "Of course, she had no idea why he wanted to take snapshots of her."

"Only three?"

"They're the best ones," said Richardson. "She really is a very pretty girl, isn't she?"

"All right," said Golly. "What's the message?"

"I don't think you made a great hit with our delicatessen friend in New York," said Richardson. "I think they were quite miffed with you."

"Too bad," said Golly.

They were past Notting Hill Gate and Kensington High Street.

"But the colonel congratulates you," said Richardson. "You were absolutely right to use those channels, in the circumstances. And that's why I am here."

"To do what?" asked Golly.

"Michael, I have taken over," said Richardson. "I am Control. As of now."

The train pulled into Earls Court.

"Let's get out," said Richardson. Two women had come into the carriage.

Outside the station, they turned right, and then right again up a side street. Golly knew that Richardson was constantly checking if he thought he saw a shadow, but he seemed reassured each time.

"You're Control?" said Golly, after they had walked in silence.

"You don't have to worry about a thing now. It's all on my shoulders. You can relax," said Richardson. "I'll pass on your orders, when necessary."

"What about John Chance?"

"Ah, John Chance," he said gently.

"Well?"

"That's why you were so right to get in touch. That's why they've sent me. John Chance is British intelligence."

58

He's like a grasshopper, thought Golly, jumping all over the place. Because suddenly Richardson waved at a passing taxi, they jumped in, and Golly heard him tell the driver:

"Avenue Road."

In the cab, Richardson made sure the sliding glass partition that separated them from the driver was shut.

"How did you know, anyway?" he asked.

"I didn't," said Golly. "I've been trying to double check, that's all."

"Lucky thing you did," said Richardson. "Your John Chance is a very clever man. Very clever indeed. Up to a point, he's been very successful. The colonel is most impressed."

"How long has he known?"

"You gave Central the tip-off, Mikhail," said Richardson. "That's why they're so pleased with you. We knew something was wrong when Hentoff was killed. That was very serious. The clever Mr. Chance nearly got away with it."

"Got away with what?"

"Hentoff was your Control," said Richardson, pulling out a Dunhill. He offered it again to Golly, who shook his head. "Of course you never knew that. He'd never had occasion to communicate with you. But he was the man who would have given you your instructions when the time came."

"How did Chance know?"

Richardson shrugged. "We'll find out. Once he knew, he killed Hentoff. Pushed him out of a window."

"Chance killed him?"

"Of course. By removing your Control, he could impersonate him."

Richardson sat back in the leather seat and smiled reassuringly at Golly.

"But now you can relax," he said. "Nothing to worry about. We're back on the rails."

"What do I do now?" asked Golly. Nothing seemed real any more. For some silly reason, his eyes kept picking up the cigarette stub stuck behind the cab driver's right ear.

"I have sent Central a full report," said Richardson, "and I expect to get instructions quite soon. If they apply to you, I will pass them on."

"You're in direct touch with Central?"

"Of course," said Richardson, rather haughtily.

"Could you do something for me?"

"What?" asked the man called Ian Richardson cautiously.

"Ask them to buy my daughter a present from me. A nice dress. A handbag. Just a present. Please."

Golly hung on his reply.

Richardson shook his head. "No," he said. "Impossible. Security must not be jeopardized."

"The message would only take a few seconds . . ." Golly was pleading.

"It must not be done," said Richardson. He said it gently. "You forget."

"What?"

"You forget that, as far as she is concerned, you're dead."

59

The cab dropped them outside the private clinic, and they walked across the road into Regent's Park. Richardson had worked his grasshopper routine into a fine art.

In the park, Richardson took Golly's arm for a moment.

"I know it's not easy, Mikhail," he said softly. "One day, the miracle will happen, when the time has come for it to happen. But until then she must continue to believe that you were killed in the car crash. When she was ten. She must always believe that, until you return."

"She doesn't have to know the present comes from me," said Golly.

"So what meaning would it have? How would one explain it? No. It must always remain a thought."

They walked for a few moments, each alone with whatever was in his mind.

"One thing," said Golly, at last. "What do I say to John Chance?"

"At the moment, you continue to play the game.

Don't let on that you suspect anything. Make him think you have accepted him as being genuine."

"It's not that easy."

"Why not? You don't see that much of him, do you? You're not supposed to be contacting him, are you?"

"No," said Golly. "He gets in touch with me."

"You know," mused Richardson. "The man is remarkable. I like the idea of his telling you blithely that he is British intelligence to try you out, and then changing his role. You don't expect the British to have such imagination. Not any more."

He pressed a button on his wrist watch. Until he did that, the face was blank. Now the time lit up, in red numerals.

"I must go, Mikhail," said Richardson. "Things to do."

"How can I reach you?" asked Golly.

"Ah, yes. Well, I know where to get you, of course. But if there are any problems, you can get me at these numbers."

He produced a piece of paper. On it, were seven phone numbers, each under one day of the week.

"Here you are," he said. "On any day, if you need me, call me at six p.m. at the right number for the right day. Don't lose it."

"What are these?" asked Golly.

He grinned. "Call boxes. In streets. On the railway stations. In hotels. A different one each day. I'll be near the right one every day at six, if you want me. I'll hear the phone ring, don't worry."

"If it's an emergency?"

"It's just have to wait until six o'clock each evening, won't it?" he said.

"I suppose so."

"One other thing. Call these numbers from a public booth. Don't use your own phone. Just in case."

He smiled at Golly.

"Don't look so worried, dear friend. The day has been saved. It was nearly a catastrophe, but you averted it. The colonel thinks your dedication is an example to all illegals. The Directorate is proud of you."

"It's a mess," said Golly.

"You've been under great strain, Mikhail. Relax. Just remember one thing, though."

Suddenly he was very grave.

"Take care with John Chance. The man is a killer. He's already murdered one of our people over here. He won't stop there, I promise you. Watch yourself. All the time, Mikhail. And, whatever you do, don't let him think you suspect anything. Otherwise, you're dead."

His eyes bored into Golly's.

"Dead," he repeated.

"Yes," said Golly.

"That it, then," said Richardson. But it was more a question than a statement. Like, do you have any questions? Anything else you want to know?

"I'll just carry on, then," said Golly.

"You do that."

Richardson glanced around. Then he nodded.

"*Au revoir,*" he said. And, quite abruptly, he walked off.

He didn't once look back.

60

He rang Sharon.

"Any messages?" he asked.

She told him exactly what he thought would have happened.

"John called. John Chance. He said it was very urgent. He wants to meet you for lunch. I said I didn't know if you'd be free, but I'd tell you if you called."

"I'll meet him," said Golly. "Did he say where?"

"An Indian restaurant. The only one in Nutford Place. One o'clock. Mike, he really sounded worried. What's up?"

"Maybe he's got problems," said Golly. "Thanks, love."

It was ten to one, but the traffic was light, and the Oasis was the only Indian restaurant, near the Edgware Road end. Curiously enough, Golly remembered it when it had sold lockshen soup and gefilte fish, but that was before the Asians came.

It wasn't busy. There were three waiters, and only one customer. The customer was sitting by the wall, at the end. John Chance.

He nodded to Golly and put away the *Herald Tribune*. He had turned it to the comics page, and the crossword.

"Glad you could make it," he said.

He wore one of his Jermyn Street shirts, and the school tie. For the first time he had spectacles on, but now he took them off and put them away.

One of the three waiters came over with two menus.

"You any good at Indian food?" asked Chance, as if he didn't have a care in the world. "Otherwise, if you'll let me . . . not that it's very good here."

"Go ahead," said Golly.

"Tandoori chicken, four quarters, dahl, peas pilaw, nan and lots of onion," rattled off Chance. His nod dismissed the waiter. The British raj in action, thought Golly.

"Now then," said Chance.

The waiter came back.

"Wine?" he leered challengingly.

"I wouldn't," said Chance to Golly, "but it's up to you."

Golly shook his head.

"Water," said Chance, and the waiter stalked off, full of disappointment.

"Wine in an Indian restaurant is living a bit too dangerously," said Chance.

He looked at Golly curiously.

"Tell me about him," he said, suddenly.

Golly had expected that, too.

169

"He says he is Control," he said simply.

"Of course," said Chance.

Golly was annoyed the way he accepted that Chance knew all about it, and didn't even pretend he didn't know about the arrival of the new man.

Chance straightened a knife, putting it more to the side, very orderly.

"And he told you that he had been sent from Central as a result of your SOS, and that I was really British intelligence," he went on.

"Yes," said Golly. No point in denying it.

"Do you believe him?" asked John Chance, and he looked at Golly keenly.

The waiter came over and put down some chutney on a little dish.

"I don't know what I believe," said Golly.

"I'll tell you about Mr. Richardson," said Chance. "He's infiltrated the apparatus. He wormed his way into the network. He's been sent on a very special assignment. He's come into his own here, on his new home territory. His job is to destroy us. He started with Hentoff. You're next on the list. Then me."

The waiter brought the dishes and placed them strategically on the table.

"*Bon appetit*," he said. He had ambitions.

"Tell me more about Richardson," said Golly.

"There's nothing more to say, is there?" said Chance. He put two red pieces of chicken on Golly's plate.

"I think there's lots more," said Golly.

Chance finished serving him.

"Not really," he said. "We now wait for what he asks you to do, and then we'll decide how we react."

"We?"

"Of course," said Chance. He munched. "It's delicious. Better than last time. Nicely spiced. Try the dahl."

"You seem to take it all very lightly," murmured Golly.

"What else do you expect me to do?" asked Chance.

The enemy, you know, and all that. At least we've tumbled to the gentleman."

Golly ate a little.

"Oh," said Chance suddenly, as if something had become clear to him. "Of course."

"What?"

"Credentials. He brought his own credentials, didn't he? Foolproof ones, right?"

"Maybe," said Golly.

"Photos of your daughter. Taken outside a theater. And in front of that big hotel. Taken in Moscow. Right?"

He beamed at Golly.

"Yes, he did."

Chance nodded.

"What better proof, eh? Very effective. She's even wearing the same clothes as in the photo I gave you."

Golly didn't have to reply.

"You see, I know," said Chance. "Central knows how the gentleman works. We're up to his tricks."

"So where did he get the pictures?" asked Golly.

"The snappy catch answer is, the same place I got mine, I shouldn't wonder."

Suddenly his face was grim.

"There is a traitor, Michael. There is somebody, right at the heart of things. *That's* why we've been penetrated."

"And who is that?" asked Golly.

"Central is on to him," said Chance. "You leave that to them. We've got enough problems."

He pushed his plate away.

"It's an interesting situation you're in," he mused. "You must really sometimes wonder if you're coming or going. We—he and I—we both seem to know it all, don't we? But only one of us is genuine. The question is—"

"I may know the answer," said Golly, very quietly.

"Ah," said Chance. "Good. I just hope it's the correct one. Because your life depends on it."

The waiter came and removed the plates. They

skipped coffee. Chance hinted it was only one degree less dangerous than the wine.

"*He* told you, of course, not to let on that you might suspect me," said Chance. "Well, I'm telling you the same about him."

"I see," said Golly.

"The interesting thing will be, then, which one of us gives you an assignment first. And what that assignment will be, right?"

Chance paid the bill.

Outside, they walked past the school playground up the street.

"Are you going to tell him about our meeting?" asked Chance innocently.

"I wouldn't be surprised if he knows already," said Golly.

"Neither would I," agreed Chance. "He's probably very well informed."

"Like you," said Golly.

They were in front of the Christian Science Church.

"Play it cool, Mikhail," said Chance.

He saw Golly stiffen.

"What's the matter?" he asked, tense.

"Across the road," said Golly tersely. "That ground-floor window. I saw something . . ."

"What?" asked Chance, looking to the other side.

"I—I think it was a camera," said Golly. "Somebody—somebody was taking a picture. Of us . . ."

Chance narrowed his eyes. Then he relaxed.

"You're seeing things, dear boy," he said.

"Somebody was there," insisted Golly.

"Take it easy," said Chance, walking on. "You'll be seeing guns with silencers next."

Golly said nothing. He wondered who would know that they'd be walking down here.

"John," he asked. "You often eat at that place?"

"Good God, no," said Chance. "I just thought it would make a change." But he had seemed to feel perfectly at home.

172

61

The light on the blue phone flashed.

"Yes?" said Foxglove. On that line, there was no need to give his identity. And he knew who'd be at the other end. It was kept clear for that purpose.

"He's having tea," said Baron's voice. "In Fortnum's. In the soda fountain."

Baron sounded really annoyed.

"So?" asked Foxglove. "What do you want us to do about it?"

"I just thought I'd report in," said Baron. "He doesn't give me much chance to get to a phone. I've never known a bloke to chase around so much."

"He is a very active gentleman," said Foxglove, "in every sense of the word. Tell me, has he spotted you?"

"Of course not," said Baron. He seemed hurt.

"You sure?"

"No, of course he hasn't," said Baron. "If there were two of us, it would be easier, naturally . . ."

"You're doing very well," said Foxglove, soothingly. "Just keep after him."

He nearly added "there's a good boy."

"I'd like to get a bite to eat, sir," said Baron.

"Why don't you join him, in the soda fountain?" said Foxglove.

At his pay phone, Baron frowned. He never was absolutely sure when this old buzzard was being sarcastic and when he meant it.

He decided to ignore it.

"What happens tonight, sir?" asked Baron.

"Tonight?"

"I've been with him since just after eight."

The voice was very reproachful.

"Oh, *that*," said Foxglove. "Don't worry, I'll arrange for you to be relieved later. Sometime this evening. Just ring in, and we'll fix a meet. Any time after nineteen-hundred hours."

But Baron did not ring in.

It was just five minutes to seven when he stood on the Northern line platform at Tottenham Court Road station.

The man he had been trailing was standing on the same platform, indistinguishable from any of the scores of other travelers waiting for the Archway train.

The man at no time appeared to have become aware that all day, all over town, Baron had doggedly, persistently, kept him within vision.

Not that it had yielded anything interesting.

The man hadn't met anyone. He hadn't picked up anything. He hadn't left anything anywhere. He had just moved around. Done some shopping. Two books in the Charing Cross Road, a tie in Mount Street, the evening paper in Leicester Square. He had had lunch in Cranbourne Street. He had walked a lot. He seemed to enjoy walking.

The indicator showed the train was coming, and already in the distance Baron could hear the rumble of the train approaching from the tunnel.

It happened very quickly, and the people on the platform didn't seem even to be aware of it at first. Baron felt somebody pushing him. So hard, he lost his balance, fell forward over the edge of the platform, onto the rails, straight in front of the onrushing train.

The driver in his cab saw a blurred figure fall almost under his carriage. He released the dead man's handle. As the emergency braking system swung into action, the wheels of the train screeched agonizingly, ground to a sudden halt, blazing off sparks.

Then somebody screamed. White-faced, the driver got out onto the platform. There wasn't much to be seen. A leg, sticking out from under the train, and a brown sock. Baron always wore brown socks. His mother bought them at birthdays and Christmastime.

They closed the Northern line for twenty minutes while firemen gathered what remained of Baron in a rubber tarpaulin, and an ambulance raced off with its sum total.

It wasn't in fact until two hours later, when a London Transport policeman in the mortuary was going through the things in Baron's jacket and trousers, that they discovered the special pass with the thick red line and the photograph and the official stamp, all of which identified the dead man as being an official of the Ministry of Defence.

In Mayfair, the duty officer took the call. He had some difficulty in tracking down Foxglove, but eventually traced him to an American film producer's home in Hyde Park Street.

"There's been an accident, sir," said the duty officer apologetically. "One of your people. From your department, I mean. Called Baron. I'm afraid he fell under a tube train at Tottenham Court Road. Killed instantly. Shocking accident, sir."

"Thank you," said Foxglove. "Only I don't think it was an accident."

"Not business at this time in the evening?" asked the hostess when Foxglove returned to the living room. She thought he was a stockbroker in New Broad Street.

"Somebody's gone sick," said Foxglove apologetically. "That was only to tell me he wouldn't be at the office in the morning."

62

He stood by the huge fifteen-inch naval-gun battery in front of the War Museum, a camera slung around his neck, a London street map in his hand, for all the world a tourist on his mandatory round.

"Hello, Ian," said Golly.

Richardson nodded. It was his idea to meet here. He had told Golly something had come up.

"Enormous, isn't it?" he said, craning his neck up at the gun. "And nothing but a peashooter."

"Not in those days," said Golly.

They went up the steps into the museum, and Golly wondered why the man had suggested this place.

Inside, Richardson seemed to know his way, and guided him to Trench Warfare.

The distant rumbling of artillery fire merged with the tramp of infantry boots and the men whistling "Mademoiselle from Armentières." It was the never-ending tape, providing background atmosphere amid the exhibits of men dying in no man's land, bodies hanging on barbed wire, soldiers sheltering in dugouts. And it provided good cover for conversation.

Especially with no one around.

"I don't know how you're going to take this, Michael," said the man called Ian Richardson. "It's really in your own interest, as much as anybody's."

You do sound so English, thought Golly. Exactly like John Chance.

"What is it?" he asked.

"Central feels it's time to reorganize things," said Richardson. He seemed to be picking his words carefully. "You know how neurotic they can get. They think that maybe things have been allowed to slide over here."

"Slide?"

They stopped by a case containing trench-fighting weapons. Vicious coshes with spiked nails sticking out, knives whose handles were also knuckle dusters, spikes to thrust into victims' eyes.

"Too cosy, perhaps," said Richardson.

"Exactly what are you trying to tell me?"

"I am only giving you Central's thinking," said Richardson. All the while he was watching Golly carefully. "They're concerned about you and the—the lady."

He was being punctiliously correct.

Golly said nothing.

"They quite understand how it's come about," said Richardson. "But it's really against the rules, isn't it?"

"What is?" asked Golly coldly. I am not going to help you, he thought. I am not going to make it easier.

Richardson's face was slightly flushed, as if he found this embarrassing.

"You and I are operational people, we know it's easy to make the rules. I know that, Mikhail. They don't have to exist in anonymous hotel rooms, wander around, desperate for warmth, human warmth, companionship. They don't know what it's like. I do."

He broke off.

"Come to the point," said Golly.

"You've got very close to this girl Sharon," he said, like somebody taking the plunge. "You've been with her, what, three years? You're married to her."

"Not really," said Golly, defensively.

"Oh, yes. You tell me the difference. And that's what's bothering Central. You used to play the field, remember? That social worker, what was her name . . . Anna. The little actress. It never lasted more than three, four months. It made everybody happy. *Everybody*. Even the Danish affair was over after seven months. She went back, didn't she?"

"You certainly have kept tabs," said Golly, bitterly.

"Central has," said Richardson. "It's the job, old son."

Old son. You and John Chance.

"Well?" said Golly. They were standing in front of sniper rifles. A hooded figure in a gas mask stared at them, a dummy dressed in chemical warfare kit.

"You've kept very quiet about Sharon," said Richardson. He paused. "You don't mind my calling her that, do you? Miss Weston sounds so formal."

"I'm sure she wouldn't care a damn," said Golly.

"I'm not enjoying this," said Richardson. His haughty face was suddenly very cold. "Don't make it more difficult for me. Instead of ringing the changes, you've chosen to get yourself permanently involved with one girl. Such an involvement is unwise. It can be dangerous. In our job, emotions can be lethal. You know that."

There was a sudden burst of machine-gun fire on the tape.

"So what am I supposed to do?" asked Golly, and his tone was hostile.

177

"Central understands the situation," said Richardson, picking his words carefully. "It is not easy for you. But you must terminate this relationship."

"Those are the orders?" said Golly. Now he was frightened. Not only for himself. For what it meant to him. But for her.

"It is left to you how you do it. But she must no longer be part of your life. If you become operational, fully operational, if you start being active, you cannot have her living in your pocket. The sleep is over, friend."

Three schoolboys came into the gallery.

"Coo, look at this one," said one, admiring the close-combat weapons. "Crash. Bang. Smash. Wow."

"I could make one of them," said the smallest one, who had spectacles. "Easy."

The other two were impressed.

"No kidding?"

They walked on, silent, fantastic thoughts of mayhem, bloodshed and violence on the Clapham bus, the south London playground and the local car park going through their minds.

Richardson watched them go.

"I suggest a trip," he said. "Get away from her. Then tell her . . . Well, you know best."

"I've just been away," said Golly.

"I don't mean that kind of trip," said Richardson. "Take leave. Pick up a woman."

His well-shaped lips formed themselves into a slight sneer; yes, he would have been at home with the Borgias.

"Do you know what you are saying?" asked Golly. "Do you actually understand what you are asking me to do?"

"It's a pity you ever allowed it to get this far. Now you're in a tangle. Of course I know that it is a sacrifice . . ."

Now the singing and the whistling of the marching troops faded, and the artillery barrage started up again.

178

Golly turned and faced him.

"Suppose I said no?"

Richardson said nothing. His eyes just kept looking at Golly.

"Supposing I said she stays. She is important to me. I can trust her. She doesn't know anything anyway, but if she did I could trust her. She stays."

"I would have to tell Central," said Richardson, very quietly. His face was now pale. In the dim light, his cheekbones stood out.

"And?"

"What do you think? It *is* an order."

"It has nothing to do with them," said Golly.

"Everything has to do with them," said Richardson.

He turned, and they walked out of the trenches.

"Michael," he said, and he used the English form. "You haven't said anything like that to me, and I haven't heard you. I have passed on Central's instructions. As Control, that is my job, the rest is with you."

Golly said nothing. They were now in the Second World War. Richardson stopped in front of a Japanese exhibit.

"Look, kamikaze pilots," he said. "Now *that* takes guts. To commit suicide in the line of duty."

He didn't give Golly a chance to reply, but strode on slowly, now and then glancing at the war relics.

Outside, he smiled at Golly.

"You know where to get hold of me, you've got the numbers," he said.

"What are you going to tell Central?" asked Golly.

"I shall report that I have passed on their instructions, and that you are proceeding to implement them," said Richardson.

"I love her," said Golly, and felt foolish saying it to this cold, aristocratic-looking face.

"You love your daughter, too," said Richardson, brutally. "And you've managed to do without her for seven years."

Golly hated him then.

"I'll wait for your progress report," said Richardson.

"Until that's cleared up, you can't really go operational. And you want to get going, don't you?"

"Yes," said Golly, "I want to get going."

Richardson nodded, pleased.

"I think we'd better make tracks," he said. "Rather, I will. Why don't you hang about a bit? Makes it less obvious."

He shot his usual quick glance around. And seemed satisfied.

"Have fun," he said, and walked off into Lambeth Road.

Golly saw him jump on a bus going toward the West End.

Have fun. Great.

Suddenly he remembered. He had read it somewhere. This place used to be Bedlam. The lunatic asylum. The real Bedlam.

Maybe it still was.

63

Of course, it wasn't just the problem of security. They wanted to be rid of Sharon for another reason. He knew that full well.

He was one of their creatures. He was allowed to have creature comforts. He could eat, get drunk, fuck, enjoy himself. But he was not allowed to have any human feelings.

In the communications room, he was a cypher. And that was what he had to be in flesh-and-blood terms.

The fact that Sharon was important to him, that he thought about her when she wasn't around, that she meant more to him than he had ever realized, all that made her dangerous.

He was not allowed to have a divided loyalty. He was not allowed to put anyone before them.

He'd been aware of the risk from the start, of course. The rules of the game had been drummed into him.

From the organization's point of view, Sharon probably did know too much already. Not a lot, but too much.

The photo, for instance. They hadn't discussed it again, but he knew that, sooner or later, the whole subject of his daughter was bound to come up.

And, no matter how guarded he was, another piece of the jigsaw puzzle might slip out. And yet another.

He knew that what was being demanded of him made sense. In their position, he would give the same order.

And in their position, he would not trust himself to obey it. Which meant that he would already be making contingency plans about himself . . .

Unless, of course . . .

John Chance appeared to be smiling at him, mockingly.

John Chance, who had never ordered him to get rid of her. Which made Golly even more afraid.

Because she knew John Chance.

And Golly knew why he was afraid of that; because she was getting involved with a man of shadows, because this was a world he wanted to keep away from her. A man she had apparently come to trust. If Chance was genuine, he was much more dangerous than Richardson to Sharon, because Chance might take advantage of her trust to deal with her himself.

Maybe that was the clue. Maybe that proved John Chance was his Control. Because Control would be anxious to know more about the girl who lived with the sleeper. Control would be anxious to meet her, find out about her. To disarm her. Maybe even get involved with her? It gave Control another string to its puppet.

Perhaps that was it. That made a great deal of sense. And would explain everything.

Yet Ian Richardson's instructions also made sense. Because Control might equally well be afraid of a sleeper becoming too intimate with an outsider. Above all, a sleeper who started to share his existence with a girl.

And obviously Central would then order him to break it off. Get rid of her.

The thing that frightened Golly more than any other was a fact that he and those like him knew only too well: there could be no disobedience. The game did not allow for it.

By refusing to break with Sharon, he might become her unwitting executioner. If he could not get rid of her, they would. If he could not do it with words, they would do it in a different way. The Second Directorate would take over. And it would be he, indirectly, who signed her death warrant.

But he could not tell her. Not what they wanted.

Sharon had to stay. She had to.

But it might mean that they both had to disappear.

64

He brought two air tickets to Rome. He left the dates of the journey open, to be booked later. But he wanted to have the security of the tickets.

He didn't know why he had picked Rome. Perhaps it was both near enough and yet sufficiently far. A springboard for the Middle East, Africa, or elsewhere in Europe. A city where he wasn't known.

If it had to happen, and they both vanished, he knew the alarm bells would start ringing. They might even suspect at first that he had defected, but then, when no ground tremors became obvious, they might accept that he really had opted out. He might be a deserter, but at least no traitor.

One safety factor was his watertight isolation; he couldn't betray all that much. Not about the present. The past, perhaps. Things that happened fifteen years back. Operational things about training, deployment, selection. But it would all be dated, and they'd know that.

It would have to be done very suddenly. One morning. A cab to the airport, and away. No milk canceled.

No good-bye parties. No hint to anyone. Maybe they'd have to tell Sharon's mother they were going on a holiday. Just to stop her getting alarmed too early.

And what would he tell Sharon? That this was the end of everything she was used to? That if she came back to England, which was doubtful, it would be as a different person, with a different name? That from now on, every stranger would be a potential enemy?

For the moment, he could push that aside. He still had to make up his mind. But he knew that would be almost the biggest problem. How to spell it out to her.

They both had passports, of course, and he also, without telling her, brought three hundred pounds worth of traveler's checks, in dollars, on each passport. He put the thick wad of checks away with the tickets. At least all that was ready. Any time. Day or night.

He wondered if he should caution her to be careful. To keep her eyes open. Just in case Central started getting impatient. They might feel that more drastic action was needed to eliminate her from his life. Something innocuous that nobody could prove was anything but an accident—say, a car that didn't stop afterward. He had seen two people knocked down and killed in London streets over the years. Who would think a third was exceptional?

But if he warned her, it would involve too many explanations.

He couldn't tell her.

But he could make sure of one thing. That when the moment came, they would be ready to disappear.

And that's exactly what he did.

65

Two days later, Richardson called him and asked him to ring him at a phone box in two hours. It annoyed Golly. He was sure it was unnecessary. Just a piece of theatricals. The man liked conspiracy. It fitted with his medieval haughtiness.

And all the phone call to the unknown booth produced was a terse order to meet at the Holiday Inn, Swiss Cottage, at 4:00 P.M.

Richardson was sitting in the lounge, picking an éclair from a large selection. He nodded to Golly.

"Which one do you want?" he asked, surveying the pastry trolley. It reminded Golly of John Chance at the Ritz.

"Nothing," said Golly curtly.

"I got you a little present," said Richardson, and he handed Golly a package, neatly wrapped in brown paper and tied with a string. It was box-shaped, and it was quite heavy.

"What's this?" asked Golly, surprised.

"A little souvenir," said Richardson. He finished the éclair rather quickly. Then he looked at Golly.

"Well, how goes it?"

Golly knew what he meant.

"It's under control."

"Yes?"

"I think she may go abroad."

"Oh, really?"

"Yes. Take a long holiday. She hasn't had one for ages. I told her if I can get away I'll come with her."

"Will you?" asked Richardson softly.

"Of course not. But it'll make things easier."

"What things?" asked Richardson, still very softly.

"The break," said Golly.

"Ah."

He seemed satisfied.

"I'll leave it all to you, then," he said.

"Is that what you wanted to see me for?" asked Golly, coldly.

"Not really," said Richardson. "Something's come up."

"Oh yes?"

"For you, Mikhail."

"What?"

"Orders," said Richardson. "There's a job to do."

So now he would know.

"Quite an interesting job," said Richardson. He looked around, but nobody was paying the slightest attention to them.

"Maybe you'd better tell me what it is," said Golly lightly. But his heart was pounding.

"Central wants you to terminate John Chance."

Richardson said it without drama. It could have been an invitation to a game of golf. If you happen to be free, old son.

Kill John Chance. Just like that.

"That's not my line," said Golly, very quietly.

Richardson nodded.

"I know there are specialists, but Central feels you're the best man for this particular assignment. After all, you know him well, he trusts you . . ."

"John Chance doesn't trust anybody," said Golly.

"You know how to get hold of him . . ."

"I don't," said Golly. "He gets in touch with me. That's how he works it."

"Oh, yes, of course. Well, I'm sure he will. Then you'll have your opportunity."

"I—I don't kill people," said Golly.

"No?" A frozen smile on the cold face. You are a liar, the smile said.

"Why kill him?" asked Golly. It seemed such a ridiculous question, here in the hotel, with the tourist party checking in at reception and people going to and fro and the world apparently quite normal.

"To protect ourselves," said Richardson. "Before he gets us. Because he's after both of us."

"If he's what you say, he needs us, doesn't he? He'll try to use us."

"Mikhail, you don't understand. He's wiping us out. What do you think happened to my predecessor? He murdered Hentoff. I've been sent to see what the hell's going on. He'll murder me. And then, when you've done your bit, he'll kill you."

"Not while I'm useful . . ."

"Wake up," said Richardson. "Maybe you've just about stopped being useful."

"I don't see—"

"It is a direct order," said Richardson. "It is not for you and me to question an order."

They were silent.

Then Golly asked:

"When am I supposed to . . . ?"

"That is up to you. But it has to happen quickly. Otherwise you and I may not be around."

"I don't know when he'll contact me next . . ."

"It'll be soon," said Richardson. "After all, he'll want to have a progress report about me, won't he?"

In the flat, Golly locked the door. Then he opened the parcel.

It was a pistol. A 7.62 mm Brigant, Czech made. Model 52, with eight rounds. And with it was an extra fitting, wrapped in tissue paper. A silencer.

Alconbury

66

They called Foxglove at six in the morning and said that the plane would be coming in at Alconbury, not Northolt.

"What time?" he asked. He was quickly awake.

"ETA 09:15," they said. "Sorry, sir."

He slammed down the phone. It was a good two hours' drive, if there were no holdups. And he had to be there.

He dialed the special number.

"Foxglove," he said. "The car that's due to pick me up at eight. I want it here in half an hour."

As he showered, he wondered why the plane had been diverted. It could hardly be the weather. It was bright, sunny outside. Northolt would be clear.

No, he guessed it was a last-minute panic at Langley. Northolt was too near London. Alconbury seemed more remote. And, anyway, it had a tradition as a spook base. In intelligence matters, the Americans were great ones for myths.

There had been a lot of high-level argument before they would even consider touching down in England.

"It's too risky," the Heidelberg office had insisted. "The sooner we shake off Europe, the safer. Once the plane lands at Andrews, we can relax. Until then . . ."

"We guarantee security," Foxglove had promised, perhaps rashly. "A black-out operation and complete security."

"Oh, sure . . ." Heidelberg had said, sounding very doubtful.

"Nothing will be left to chance," said Foxglove.

"You know how hot this cargo is," said Heidelberg. "They'll do anything to get at it. Anything. It's the biggest catch we've had since Helsinki."

Foxglove couldn't recall what it was that they had caught at Helsinki, but he agreed. The cargo was a prime target.

Inwardly, he thought that only Americans would call a man cargo.

"Well, I don't know," Heidelberg had signed off. "We'll think about it. I'll send you a Telex, of course."

So Foxglove rushed over to Old Marylebone Road and saw Crayton.

"It's as much in your interest as ours, surely," he had pointed out. "It affects both of us . . ."

"You're taking a hell of a risk, Gerry," Crayton said. "If it goes wrong . . ."

"We're been taking a risk the whole time with this bloody thing," said Foxglove.

"Well," agreed Crayton, who had come as a Rhodes Scholar and stayed to head a very special American intelligence section, "it seems to have worked so far."

"But it's all wasted unless they'll co-operate now," pleaded Foxglove.

"Okay," said Crayton. "I'll throw in my two cents' worth."

Langley didn't like it one bit. They wanted their hands on the cargo quickly. But Crayton had also enlisted an ally at the Embassy, and even Jackson of ONI committed himself, for once.

"I agree this is in the interest of the United States," Jackson had said portentously.

So, after some more top-secret enciphered communications between a certain signals facility at Landstuhl in Germany, the radio room in Grosvenor Square, and a microwave station in West Virginia, agreement came:

"The British can have the cargo for twenty-four hours."

Then came the little matter of where the cargo would land. Foxglove had suggested three suitable RAF bases. Heidelberg, holding the cargo in its hot hands, insisted on a U.S. installation. Langley upheld Heidelberg. Crayton proposed Mildenhall. After all, the cargo would have to go on from Mildenhall anyway. Langley thought something more remote and less busy, like Wethersfield. Heidelberg suggested Northolt.

That was last night.

The buzzer went, and Foxglove knew that his driver was downstairs. The car was black, anonymous, and you had to look twice to see the radiotelephone.

"Alconbury," said Foxglove to the driver, who had spent fourteen years in Special Air Service and still looked the part. "It's an American air base."

"Yes, sir, I know it," said Bolton, the driver. "Near Huntingdon."

"I have to be there by nine o'clock at the latest," said Foxglove.

Bolton glanced at the car clock.

"We'll be there," he promised, swinging the car into Palace Gate.

Bolton spoke only once on the trip.

"I have the *Guardian* and the *Financial Times*, if you want them, sir," he said.

"Yes, please," said Foxglove. SAS men always pulled surprises.

Bolton reached over with the two papers.

"There you are, sir," he said, keeping his eyes on the road.

"Thank you," said Foxglove, genuinely grateful.

At least it made up for not having had time for two three-minute eggs.

67

Twenty-eight thousand feet up, the executive jet with the U.S. Air Force markings streaked toward its destination, radar eyes following it every second.

It was a small, comfortable plane and, inside, a master sergeant, impeccably white-jacketed, moved around, quietly pouring coffee for the three passengers whenever their cups ran low.

The jet belonged to the general's flight at Lindsey, and its interior was tastefully designed, from the individual reading lamps to the discreet gray upholstery.

The three passengers were in civilian clothes, and two of them were armed. Their small leather holsters, with the stubby guns, were concealed by their jackets.

The cargo sat silent, reading *Playboy* and *The New Yorker*. He had been surprised to find a *Playboy* on a VIP plane, and he didn't find *The New Yorker* very funny.

A full colonel sat at the controls, and his co-pilot was a captain from one of the Special Flights at Landstuhl. The captain had fourteen hundred hours in U2's to his credit, and was one of the few men who had flown over Manchuria seven times.

The colonel did not normally pilot aircraft. He usually sat behind a desk, reading reports that were invariably classified Top Secret. And some of the things he did as a result were so delicate that they were not even committed to paper, no matter how high their security grading. But he had wings and he had to get in some flying time, and he was the right man to be in charge of the flight. He, after all, knew it all.

Officially, the plane had no escort. But in the distance, to starboard, three Phantoms kept respectfully astern, and although their crews did not know much about it, they had been told that nothing, repeat nothing, must happen to the silver jet.

Above all, no strangers must intrude into its air corridor.

From one to the other, the military air-control centers passed the jet like a relay baton. And when Anglia Control picked it up on the screen, it was almost home.

"Blue One on course," reported the captain, who had taken over the console. In the cool, air-conditioned control center in Suffolk, where, at any one time, two dozen aircraft were being monitored as they came in and out of the traffic zone, everyone knew Blue One must be special.

It even had a flight corridor all to itself, with no other plane allowed to approach within five miles.

"Some big shot?" asked the RAF squadron leader, who, as liaison officer with Third Air Force, was supposed to know everything.

"Guess so," said the traffic controller, chewing the gum he had in his mouth only when he was watching something special on the screen. Normally, he chewed an unlit cigar.

"Blue One making its approach turn."

"Blue One, you're right on beam," said the controller.

"I wonder who it is?" said the squadron leader. It annoyed him when the Yanks became so taciturn. After all, Anglia Control was basically a British facility that the Americans had on loan.

If it had been a Galaxy or one of those monster transports that descend on certain bases in England periodically, it would probably have meant a Rodeo flight.

Rodeo meant nuclear weapons. The Air Force flew them in under conditions of great secrecy, and the planes were shepherded like children crossing a busy road.

But Blue One was only a little executive jet. The kind Frank Sinatra used. The kind American generals had at their disposal.

Inside the plane, the cargo looked out of one of the

portholes. They were beginning to break cloud, and the island was below them. Green fields. Long roads. Farmhouses. This part was very rural. Very flat.

"More coffee, sir?" asked the master sergeant.

The cargo shook his head.

The two armed men in civilian clothes said nothing. They wished it wasn't Alconbury they were coming in to. If it was Andrews, their responsibility would be over and they could relax.

But until the cargo got safely to Andrews, they were, as they had been briefed, in the hot seat.

The cargo seemed to be unconcerned.

"How much longer?" he asked.

One of the men looked at his watch.

"Touchdown in ten minutes," he said.

"Good," said the cargo. "Let's get it over."

68

They stopped Foxglove's car at the gate to the big, sprawling base and phoned through to make sure that he was expected.

Then an Air Police car, its big radio antenna waving in the breeze, led the way and guided them past office buildings and barracks and hangars on to the complex of runways and flight lines.

A mile from the control tower, on runway three, a small group was waiting: two Air Force staff cars, a couple of civilian automobiles, and an Air Police jeep.

Foxglove got out and walked over to group. Crayton was there and came toward him.

"Morning, Gerald," he said. "You made good time. He's not due for a few minutes."

He took Foxglove by the arm and introduced him to some of the others.

"You know Jackson, of course," he said. Foxglove was surprised to see him there. ONI liked to stay out of these things. Curiosity made him come, probably.

"Colonel Geiger, from headquarters," said Crayton. The colonel wore a sports jacket. Cashmere. Flannels. Handsewn shoes. Foxglove wondered which head-quarters.

"Collins. Van Der House. Gavrinski." Crayton rattled off the names.

By God, they do look identical, thought Foxglove. The same button-down shirts. The same casually smart suit. The same ties, virtually.

"Mr. Foxglove represents our British friends," said Crayton. "For the next twenty-four hours, it's their show, really."

Foxglove wondered if that was by way of explanation or a subtle reminder to him that there was a time limit. A definite set time limit.

The colonel had a little two-way radio, and it suddenly started to crackle. He held it to his ear and listened.

"Roger," he said. He looked around.

"He's coming in," he said. pointing south. "Three o'clock."

Foxglove couldn't see anything. He could not even hear a plane.

"There he is," said the man called Collins.

Foxglove squinted into the sky.

Yes. Now he could see it. A small dot. Coming nearer, lowering rapidly.

Along the runway, like well-rehearsed actors, two fire trucks appeared, and an ambulance.

"Taking no chances, are you?" said Foxglove.

"Precious cargo," said Crayton.

And in the distance, Air Police jeeps had drawn a circle, cutting off the runway from idle air mechanics who might be drawn to watch the arrival of Blue One.

And suddenly the plane was there, in front of them. It bumped down very gently, taxied to a perfect halt. The pilot knew his job.

One of the jeeps raced up, and two airmen put some steps under the door of the cabin.

They began to walk toward it.

The door opened.

One of the men with a gun under his jacket appeared, looked around to satisfy himself, and then nodded to people behind him. He jumped agilely down onto the tarmac.

The cargo appeared.

He looked smartly dressed. He wore a raincoat.

Colonel Geiger stepped forward, held out his hand. "Nice to see you," he said. Crayton nodded to Foxglove.

Foxglove went up to the man in the raincoat.

"Welcome to England, Viktor Fedorovitch," said Foxglove.

69

"I don't want any part of it," said Viktor Fedorovitch. "It is not part of the bargain."

They were in Foxglove's car, racing back to London. Bolton kept his eye on the road, and had taken no objection to Foxglove's closing the glass partition.

"It is all part of the bargain," said Foxglove. "Believe me, major."

"I was told I would be flown straight to America," said the major. "I would not be debriefed in Europe. I was promised that."

"You are quite right," said Foxglove. "That is exactly how it will be done."

"Then why have I been brought here?" asked the major. "Why this stop-off in England?"

"There is a very important service you can perform for us," said Foxglove.

He felt annoyed, pleading with this man, trying to persuade him like a reluctant bride. When he had worked with Deception, they told enemy agents what to do; they didn't beg.

The major grunted.

"What exactly is involved?" he asked finally.

"Very little," said Foxglove.

"I may refuse to co-operate," said the major loftily.

"We would find that very disappointing," said Foxglove. "All of us. Including our American friends."

The major bared his teeth.

"My friend, I have enough information in here"—he tapped his forehead—" to keep you all busy. That is the price I pay. I do not need to do anything else. If you make it difficult for me, I may start getting a little amnesia."

Foxglove smiled approvingly.

"Of course, Viktor Fedorovitch. And, as you will appreciate, if you make it difficult for us, we too may become a little forgetful."

The major nodded. It was language he understood.

"Where are we going?" he asked.

"A pleasant little place. You'll only stay one night. Put your feet up."

"I would prefer to put my feet up in America. It is three thousand miles farther away. I would be happier."

The major looked out of the car window. Then he glanced through the rear window.

"We have no escort," Viktor Fedorovitch observed disapprovingly.

Foxglove seemed surprised. "No," he said.

Viktor Fedorovitch frowned.

"I don't like that," he grumbled. "We should have an escort. Where is my bodyguard. Are you armed?"

"Good God, no," said Foxglove.

"Is your man?" He nodded at Bolton through the glass.

"I wouldn't think so for a moment."

"Are you mad?" snapped the major. "Do you realize the danger I am in? Do you realize the risk you are taking—with *my life*?"

"You're perfectly safe," said Foxglove.

"The Americans give me two escorts. The whole time. Armed. One sleeps outside my door. He goes with me everywhere."

"The Americans do it differently," said Foxglove.

"This place you're taking me to, is it guarded?"

"I don't think anybody will be able to get at you there," said Foxglove. Really, the man was a pest.

"At least, I should have a gun," stormed Viktor Fedorovitch. "I do not like being a pigeon."

"Nobody could ever mistake you for one," murmured Foxglove.

"It is your responsibility," growled the major, and lapsed into sullen silence.

Then he closed his eyes. Foxglove studied him. The slightly Slavonic cast of features. The hair beginning to turn gray at the temples. The lines that gave his mouth a cruel downward twist.

This, then, was the man in charge of Special Activities. The man code-named Odin until they had established his identity. The man who had sent Summers and Wilson and the girl Gresham to their deaths. The man who operated the illegals . . .

Foxglove found the major's open eyes staring at him. He felt himself going red.

"You have my habit, Mr. Foxglove," said the major. "Studying people when they are not aware of it. Well, what did you think? How do you analyze me?"

"I think you are a quite dangerous man, Viktor Fedorovitch," said Foxglove.

"Not to you. Not any more. That is over, my friend."

He pulled out a Dunhill pack.

"At least I will be able to get as many of these as I want," he said.

Foxglove lit it for him.

"Tell me," he asked, "how is the colonel?"

"Not very happy, I imagine."

"I can understand that."

Viktor Fedorovitch blew out some smoke.

"I imagine he will do his best to make sure that I am dead quite soon."

He looked out of the window.

"Where is this, precisely?"

"It is called Hampstead," said Foxglove.

"Oh, yes. The highest suicide rate in London."

"Really?" said Foxglove. "I didn't know."

"I read it in some digest of statistics. And Sunday is the peak day. You must forgive me. I have this ridiculous habit of collecting odd facts and storing them in my memory."

"It is not ridiculous at all," said Foxglove. "It's your job really, isn't it?"

"*Our* job," said Viktor Fedorovitch, and smiled. "Perhaps we don't have minds at all. Just attics stuffed with old newspapers."

"Old newspapers can be very useful," said Foxglove.

"I just had an interesting thought," said the major.

"Tell me."

"I wondered if our roles were reversed—if you were sitting in my car, being driven through a Moscow suburb, with me as your host—if we would also be talking about old newspapers. If you were in my position, so to speak."

"Ah," said Foxglove, "but you see, my dear major, you are not in my position."

Viktor Fedorovitch turned his head and looked out of the window.

"Where are we now?" he asked.

"Still Hampstead."

After that, the major lapsed into silence. But he looked a little uneasy.

70

In a nine-story annex a mile east of the Baltimore-Washington expressway, a ten-million-dollar computer was humming gently as it came up with 229,000 variations a second on a group of figures that had been fed into it by a taciturn cryptography analyst. The building, ringed by three fences of five-strand electrified wire, guarded by armed Marines, was the cypher-busting nerve center of NSA, which some called the National Security Agency, but others knew really meant Never Say Anything.

The analyst wore a red plastic identity badge, with his photo and name. The color was important, because only red badges could enter this, the most secret section of a building where everyone was watched by closed-circuit eyes, even when they flushed the toilet.

Red badge could do little but wait. For, as always, this was really a duel between two machines—one, in a rather similar building an hour's drive from Moscow, and the other here, Fort George G. Meade, in Maryland. It was machine talking to machine, one trying to break the secrets of the other.

The message had been intercepted an hour previously, and was identified as Gorgon, the highest-level Soviet cipher system. They had been waiting for it in Langley, in Washington, in an office in Mayfair, and in a barrack-like building in Heidelberg.

Only red badges were allowed to handle it, and even the mere intercept, before PROD, the analysis department, had actually got down to the job of making the computers cough up its meaning, had been flashed to certain people as a Priority One.

It was difficult to break, although it was basically a very short message. For its cipher had been designed especially to frustrate those who were no longer gentlemen and read other people's mail.

But, after thirty-five minutes, they had the text. A text intended to be seen only by the eyes of one man in the Soviet Embassy in Kensington Palace Gardens, in the Soviet Consulate in New York, and one other place. Not even the confidential cipher clerks would know the contents, for a Gorgon message could only be decoded by the man for whom it was intended.

The message said:

"Comet has defected. Cease activity."

Comet was the cipher name of Viktor Fedorovitch.

"I think we should meet," said John Chance.

On the phone, his voice was not unlike Ian Richardson's. Very English. Very cool.

"Yes," said Golly.

"Say in an hour. At Centre Point."

"Where?"

"Centre Point. Tottenham Court Road."

"Why there?"

"I might rent some space there. On the seventh floor. Just tell the man you're meeting me."

"All right," said Golly.

"See you shortly," said Chance, and rang off.

Golly looked at his watch. Richardson wouldn't be near his phone booth until six o'clock. No way of reaching him before then.

In any case, what was the point? He had his orders. Kill John Chance.

He got the pistol out of the locked drawer. Even with the silencer screwed into the barrel, it was a short, compact little weapon. It was loaded, and it would make very little noise. He knew that. Just a plop.

It would be as silent as the gun that killed the contact in New York. So silent he did not even know the man had been shot as he sat beside him.

He held the pistol in his hand and wondered if he could go through with it. In his mind's eye, he saw the bullet hole, the reddish stain spreading across the Jermyn Street shirt, perhaps even marking the Westminster tie.

He wasn't sure, of course, if it would be the right place. Somebody would see him enter the building. And leave afterwards. Then, when Chance's body was found, it would be easy for the police . . .

On the other hand, he could make sure the janitor didn't see too much of his face. And there was bound to be some emergency exit, a fire escape, a back door, a goods lift. He could probably leave by some other way, unnoticed.

But it was risky.

He kept saying it to himself, and he knew that, really, he was trying to find an excuse to avoid the final decision. He didn't want to kill.

Perhaps it would be easier with an anonymous, shadowy figure. That's why hit men could carry out their contracts so unemotionally. The victim meant nothing to them. Sometimes they didn't even know who it was.

But John Chance . . .

He was pretty certain in his own mind that Chance was the enemy. Richardson had the brand of the organization on him. He sounded right. He felt right.

There was something about his cold eyes, the way they seemed to be looking at something else while they were staring at you. He had seen eyes like that in the building at Dzerzhinsky Square when he had first been selected.

Kazakov, who killed the Ukrainian priest in Frankfurt, had those eyes. Griboyedov had them, and people still remembered them when they had forgotten what a blue sky looked like. And Timiryazev, who destroyed the American naval attaché's wife in Oslo to get her husband's copy of the NATO battle order, had them.

And Richardson knew it all. He was the man they had sent. He was sure of that.

Which meant that John Chance was British intelligence.

Yet he kept having that nagging doubt. Curiously enough, Chance had never asked him much. He hadn't probed. He hadn't ordered him to do anything. He had just kept tabs on him, warned him, and—and he had been seeing Sharon secretly. But that was really all.

Then, suddenly, Golly had the frightening thought: Why the sudden meeting? Why did John Chance want to see him in such a tall building, on the seventh floor? Must be eighty, ninety feet above street level.

It came to him so clearly now.

Hentoff. The man who had been Control. Who died. Falling from a tall building. Pushed. Murdered by John Chance. So said Richardson.

And now John Chance, the man who liked tea at the Ritz and went to boxing matches, wanted to meet him in the most unlikely place—seven floors up.

"I might rent some space there . . ."

That's what he had said.

So that was it. A meeting no one knew about. In an empty place. High up above the street. An open window . . .

He would eliminate the sleeper.

And then it would be Richardson's turn.

Control would be wiped out.

Michael Golly stood up. He put the gun in his jacket pocket.

He knew he had to kill John Chance if he wanted to live.

72

"Why here?" asked Golly.

The room was completely bare, with wires hanging from the center of the ceiling and holes in the wall for light points. It had the musty smell of a place that had been empty for years.

"Here?" repeated John Chance. The question seemed to surprise him.

"Why meet up here? In this place?"

Chance's footsteps echoed dully as he paced from one wall to the other, apparently checking the length.

"I'm thinking it might make a nice little office. Don't you?"

"For what?"

"I might be opening a business. Something very respectable. Like a public relations firm. Only a small thing, you understand."

"Why?" Golly was watching him narrowly.

"We illegals have to do very legal things, don't we?" John Chance smiled.

"Look how well your toy business has worked out. You showed a 7,258-pound profit last year, didn't you?"

The man knew everything. "Before tax," said Golly.

"Very impressive," said Chance. He cocked his head to one side. "I could put a secretary there, in the corner, couldn't I?"

He looked around.

"Well, what do you think of it?"

"Isn't it going to cost a lot, an office in this place?" asked Golly. What a ridiculous question to ask of a man you are about to kill, he thought.

"Oh, come on, Mikhail, money is no object in this exercise."

He scratched his chin thoughtfully, as if contemplating the possibilities. Then, almost like a man whose mind was on something else, he said casually:

"Why don't you open the windows? It's a bit stuffy in here."

The moment was coming, said Golly to himself. He felt reassured by the weight of the pistol.

"Let's have some fresh air," said Chance. He had his back to Golly.

Now. Shall I do it now? He reached for his pocket.

John Chance swung around.

"Don't you think?" he added, a delayed-action completion of his statement.

Golly felt himself sweating. No. Not while he is looking at me. He walked over to the windows, tried a handle. It was stuck fast. Through the dirty glass, he could see Charing Cross Road below, the roofs of the red double-deck buses, the junction with Oxford Street.

"They won't open," said Golly.

He turned quickly to face Chance.

"Damn," said Chance. "Let me try."

He moved over to the window. Golly strategically stepped away. Well away. If you think you can do it with a sudden push, you're a fool, Chance . . . I won't be standing there, I promise you.

Chance tried hard to get the windows to budge.

"I wonder when somebody last touched these," he said.

He seemed to give up the effort.

"Maybe we can have a look at the roof," he said. "There must be a marvelous view. We'll get some air up there."

Golly said nothing.

Chance came toward him.

"Well?" he said. "Should I take it?"

Golly shrugged.

"Mikhail," said John Chance, very quietly.

His tone froze Golly.

"You are carrying a gun," said Chance.

Golly's eyes never left him.

"Why, old son?" asked Chance.

Golly licked his dry lips. He didn't know what to do. Pull the gun out now? Shoot him here, as he stood in the middle of the room?

Chance came nearer. "Tell me," he said, "is it for me? Are you going to kill me?"

Golly stared at him.

"I . . ." The words petered out. He put his hand in his pocket. He felt the cold, solid butt of the pistol.

"On our friend's instructions? Did he give you the assignment? 'Kill John Chance, he is the other side'?"

Golly nodded.

Chance stopped opposite him.

"Well," he said. "Are you going to do it?"

Golly found himself with the pistol in his hand, pointing it at the other man.

Chance nodded, as if it fit into place.

"Go ahead," he said. "Nobody will hear that silencer."

Golly's hand shook slightly.

"It may interest you to know that I have nothing. No gun. Nothing." Chance seemed quite unruffled. "I thought he'd give you the job. That's why I wanted to see you. To find out. But, as you see, I've taken no precautions."

He held open the two sides of his blue blazer with the brass buttons.

"Look," he said. "Still want to use that?"

The gun in Golly's hand wavered slightly.

"You see, old friend, I trust you," said Chance.

"You killed Hentoff," said Golly. "You were going to kill me. Like Hentoff. A quick push and it's all over."

"Through a window that doesn't even open?" said Chance. "Give me a little credit. Don't you think I would have checked first?"

Golly lowered his gun hand a little.

"I think you've got a bit mixed up, Mikhail," said Chance, amiably. "You say I want to kill you. It's you who have come here with that thing, not me."

He shook his head.

"Didn't I tell you Richardson was dangerous?" he said. "Didn't I tell you he divides and conquers?"

He looked at his watch.

"As a matter of fact, there's a little surprise waiting for you," he said.

Golly looked arond.

"No," said Chance. "Not here. We'll have to take a little drive. Then you'll know everything. You'll know what it's all about. And you'll know, once and for all, who I am."

"Just like that," said Golly. "A little drive."

John Chance seemed annoyed, for the first time.

"Oh, for heaven's sake," he said. "You can keep your bloody gun. You can have it trained on me the whole time. You're afraid of your own bloody shadow, Mike."

The door of the empty room suddenly opened and a man stood there, in dungarees.

"Everything all right, gentlemen?" he asked. He looked at them both without curiosity.

"Yes," said John Chance. "Thank you."

"Anything you want me to show you?" asked the man.

"The windows are stuck," said John Chance.

"Well, you know the place's been empty for ages," said the man. "That can be fixed."

John Chance turned to Golly.

"Anything else you want to see, Michael?"

Golly shook his head. He hoped the man hadn't seen the gun he hastily shoved into his pocket.

"That's it, then," said Chance. "Here are the keys." He handed them to the man, a little bunch with a paper tag attached by a piece of string. "I'll let the estate agent know."

"Thank you," said the man in dungarees.

"Shall we go?" said Chance, and led the way out of the place. He didn't seem to worry about turning his back on Golly.

Outside they walked down the corridor to the lift.

The man in dungarees stood by the door and watched them get into the lift that would take them to the ground floor and the entrance in St. Giles Circus.

His name was Woodham, and he was a Special Branch officer.

73

The Harrys were out in New Oxford Street, a snake of them weaving and chanting, beating drums, bashing tambourines, wearing dirty saffron robes and Mohican scalp locks, yawling "Hare Krishna . . . Hare Krishna . . . Hare Krishna . . . Hare Krishna . . . Hare Hare . . . Hare Rama Rama Rama . . ."

"Bloody racket," snarled John Chance, but whether he meant the chanting or the fellowship of their worthy lordships Shree, Radha, and Krishna as an institution, he didn't make clear.

"Two things I hate about this country," he fumed,

leading the way to the mini. "Bloody royal garden parties and the traffic jams they cause, and those twits."

He's cool, thought Golly. Really cool. A few moments ago, I had a gun on him and he knew he was under sentence of death. Now he doesn't seem to have a care in the world.

"Where are we going?" asked Golly.

"Hendon," said Chance, swinging the mini round. He ignored the parking ticket a meter maid had stuck under his windscreen wiper.

"Why Hendon?"

"This seems to be your day for asking damn fool questions," said Chance. But his words belied his mood. He appeared to be in increasingly good temper. "What's wrong with Hendon?"

"Nothing," said Golly. "It's got a police college, an airfield, and Hendon Central. None of it I find very inspiring."

"You will," said Chance.

They drove in silence, but at one set of traffic lights, the red went against the mini and Chance turned to Golly.

"Got your gun nice and handy, Mikhail?" He grinned. "Enough bullets?"

He seemed to enjoy the joke hugely.

A little farther on, he asked, "How's Sharon?"

You've got a nerve, said Golly to himself. You're so damn cocksure of yourself you can't even leave her out of it. You really think I haven't found out, don't you?

"She's all right," he answered aloud, curtly.

"You're very lucky to have somebody like that. I don't know if you deserve it," said Chance, quite matter of fact.

"That's up to her, isn't it?" snapped Golly. I'm not going to have you sit in judgment, you bastard.

Chance nodded. He saw a police motorcyclist ahead and slowed down his speed slightly.

"Are you married, John?" asked Golly unexpectedly. Chance smiled thinly.

"We lose those attachments in our world," he said. "You should know that. It's one of the requirements of our tradecraft."

The back of Golly's neck prickled. Tradecraft. *That* word. The inside word. Like "nonwitting." For an outsider. Somebody who is not privileged to know. CIA slang.

Chance glanced at him.

"Yes," he said. "I like those words they use. 'Tradecraft' has a flavor all its own. Like *'nyet kulturny.'* I suppose it's *nyet kulturny* of us not to speak Russian. But since it's not the mother tongue of either of us, English makes much more sense, don't you think?"

"I suppose so," said Golly carefully.

"After all, you don't speak Russian with Mr. Richardson either, do you?"

"No."

"Of course not. Russian isn't his mother tongue, either. I suppose, in a way, we're all outsiders. Even you."

"Who are insiders?"

John Chance shrugged.

"Who indeed? I suppose Central. They may give outsiders ranks. But they stay outsiders. It's when you get to Central's level that you're on the inside. The colonel. The major. They're insiders."

He screeched to a halt as an old woman defiantly stood on the zebra crossing, waiting for them to brake.

"You trained under the major, didn't you?" asked Chance.

"He was one of the instructors. He was a lieutenant then, in the First Directorate," said Golly.

"Now Viktor Fedorovitch *is* Central. Responsible only to the colonel."

Golly nodded.

"And no outsider." Chance smiled.

They had turned into a maze of small suburban streets.

The mini pulled up in front of a fittingly small suburban house. It was not at all what Golly had expected. Its television aerial was slightly askew.

As he got out of the car, he saw the street sign. "Bertram Road" it said.

He was glad he had the gun.

74

They walked up the tiny garden path, and the front door of the house opened without their having to knock.

A man in a rolltop sweater nodded to them.

"Come in, Nicolai Stepanovich," he said to John Chance.

Nicholas Stephen?

"No," said Chance. "Here, I am John Chance."

"Of course, sir," said the man in the sweater. He held the door for Golly.

"Is he here?" asked Chance.

"On your right," said the man. "Just down the corridor."

Then he stood in front of Golly.

"Excuse me," he said very politely. "Are you armed?"

"It's all right," said Chance.

The man immediately stood to one side.

"I'm sorry," he said to Golly.

The room was small, like everything in the house.

The major sat on the sofa, drinking lemon tea. As soon as they entered, he stood up. He ignored Chance, but he went toward Golly, hands outstretched.

"Mikhail Pyotr, how wonderful to see you, dear comrade," he beamed, and embraced Golly. He kissed him on each cheek.

For Golly, the years stood still.

"I don't believe it," he said. "Viktor Fedorovitch— I don't believe it."

"Come, dear friend," said the major, "come and sit by me."

"I think," said John Chance, very tactfully, "I will leave you two to it. You must have a lot to talk about."

He walked out, closing the door gently.

"You," said Golly. "Here. In London."

"I know," nodded the major. "It seems impossible. But as you can see, I am here."

He looked at Golly affectionately.

"We are so proud of you, Mikhail," he said. "The whole section. All these years, so faithful, so loyal."

"I—I have done nothing," muttered Golly.

"You have lived up to the finest tradition of the service," said the major. "It is not your fault things got disorganized. That is why I am here."

"That man out there—John Chance. He is the other side, I think," Golly suddenly felt very insecure.

But the major smiled.

"Nicolai Stepanovich?" he said, "the other side? That man is a hero. He has carried the whole network here. He *is* carrying the whole network. You are lucky to have such a man to rely on."

"Then he—he is . . ."

Golly felt sick.

The major nodded. "I understand. It has been a bad situation. Such confusion must not arise again. The procedures for deep illegals are being urgently revised. But we have a very dangerous crisis here. That is why I have had to come."

He took a sip of his lemon tea.

"Mikhail," he said urgently, "I can only be here for twenty-four hours. That is already very risky. But we must immediately deal with this man who calls himself Ian Richardson. It is so important that I have taken charge."

"Richardson has asked me to kill—Control." Golly felt dry.

"Of course," said the major. "That is the whole object of his exercise. The man is SIS. The Devil knows how they infiltrated him. It has already cost us the life of a good comrade."

"Hentoff?"

"He was the first. You are next—after you have killed John Chance."

"But he knows everything," said Golly. "He knows names. Even the kind of cigarettes the colonel smokes. He has photos of my daughter . . ."

"I took those," said Viktor Fedorovitch. "For John Chance to give you, as credentials. But the SIS has somebody in the section. He sent the same credentials to Mr. Richardson. To convince you he was genuine."

But something else was suddenly more important to Golly.

"Viktor Fedorovitch, how is she? How is my daughter?"

The major's face broke into a sunny smile.

"She is wonderful, dear friend. The loveliest girl. Intelligent. Kind. She is growing up to be a wonderful citizen."

He looked suddenly sad.

"There is only one thing I am sorry about."

"What is it?" asked Golly anxiously.

"That she does not know what important work her father is doing for the country."

"But what have I done?"

"Dug yourself in so deep that even a mole could not find you, Mikhail. The perfect illegal undercover. Priceless to us."

"There's something you should know," said Golly.

"Please tell me."

"I live with a woman."

The major raised his hand. "The pretty Sharon. I know all about her. John Chance sings her praises."

"He does?" Golly was not quite sure how he felt about that.

"He has met her, of course, as you know. He had to make sure. He thinks she is marvelous. You have good taste, my friend."

"The man Richardson says I must get rid of her."

"But of course. What do you expect? He is set to destroy everything. You, for one. It is easier to deal with you when she is not around."

"Then Central does not want her out of the way?" asked Golly. Suddenly, it all seemed so clear.

"Why should we?" asked the major. "It is true we disapprove of illegals getting emotionally entangled. But she is a special girl."

He put his hand on Golly's shoulder.

"Our blessings, Mikhail. I speak for the organization."

All at once, the load seemed to be lifted off Golly's shoulders. It made sense.

"This Richardson. What about him? What will you do?"

"I have to make my decision," said the major. "Regretfully. He must be eliminated. Before he destroys more of us. There is no way out. Mikhail, you must remove him."

Golly thought of the irony of it. The hunter hunted. The executioner executed.

"That is not really my field, assassination," he said.

"I agree," said the major, morosely. "But tell me. Who else is there? Whom he trusts? Who can get near him? Who can find him? And you do know where to find him, don't you?"

Golly nodded.

There was a knock at the door.

"Enter," said the major.

John Chance came in. He looked from one to the other.

"Well, Mike," he said, "now you know it all."

"Yes," said Golly, thoughtfully.

"I have given our good comrade his orders and he has responded with the true courage I would expect from him," said the major.

I have? Have I really, thought Golly.

"I'm afraid there's no choice," said John Chance, full of sympathy. "He's got to be got rid of. Everybody is in danger. Even Sharon."

And that was true. Richardson had made that clear, his face flushed, his high cheekbones making him look more evil than usual.

Even Sharon was in peril.

"All right," said Golly. "I'll do it."

"How do you get hold of him?" asked the major.

John Chance said nothing. He merely waited.

"I have some phone numbers where I can reach him. A different call box every evening," said Golly.

"Every evening?" asked John Chance.

"Have you got a number for tonight?" said the major softly.

Golly had the piece of paper in his small pocket diary.

"Here," he said. "That's the number for tonight at six. But I have no idea where the call box is. He doesn't give me the location."

"I think I can find out," said John Chance, taking the paper.

"Good," said the major. "You will be there, at six. And you will kill him."

75

He stood in the alley, opposite the Greek Orthodox church, waiting. It was ten minutes to six.

It had taken John Chance less than a quarter of an hour to pinpoint the place.

"There are two phone boxes in Moscow Road, outside the telephone exchange," he said. "Next to the Greek church. This number is one of them."

Moscow Road.

"He has a sense of humor, our murderous friend," said John Chance.

"It's not exactly the loneliest place," said Golly.

"It won't take a second. He won't be expecting it. You shoot, he falls, you walk away quickly—you'll be round the corner in no time."

"Suppose somebody is passing?"

"Nobody will take the slightest notice," said Chance, reassuringly. "The English don't. They're so embarrassed by something unusual they look the other way. Didn't you read about the man who was shot down in the pin-table arcade?"

Golly wasn't really interested.

"Three people wanted their money back because the commotion made them lose their balls."

He snorted with delight.

Golly watched him silently.

"What will the others do?" he asked.

"The others?"

"Richardson's people."

"Our friends won't do a damn thing," said John Chance. "They'll know it was us who did it, and they'll chalk it up. But that's all."

"And I'm blown," said Golly. "Finished."

"We'll look after you," promised John Chance. "They know about you anyway now, don't they? I mean, you don't think Mr. Richardson will keep it to himself?"

"Do you know anything about him?" Golly was curious. After all, he had only ninety minutes left to live before he'd pull the trigger.

"I think he works for a man called Foxglove," said Chance.

"And he is . . ."

"Oh, he's their . . ." he looked around, as if he could pluck an example out of the air. "He's their Viktor Fedorovitch."

Golly was silent.

"What will happen to me?" he asked finally.

"You and Sharon will be well taken care of," said Chance. "I'll give you some time to get clear. Then I'll pick you up at your place. Both of you."

"And?"

"Tomorrow you'll both be sleeping in a different bed," said Chance.

"What time will you come?"

"Seven-thirty," said Chance. "Have your things ready. Just a suitcase each. Leave the rest."

Chance dropped him in Orme Square. They could see the policeman standing guard outside the Soviet Consulate, farther up the Bayswater Road.

"Good luck, Mikhail," said Chance. Then he drove quickly toward Notting Hill Gate.

Golly walked slowly through the small side street into Moscow Road. He could see the two red phone kiosks. He walked past them, on the other side of the road, and turned into the alley . . .

In his pocket was the gun. Silencer fitted. The gun he had nearly used once already today.

He looked at his watch. Two minutes to six. A huge coach loaded with package-tour Swedes lumbered past. Otherwise, Moscow Road was quiet. The doors of the Greek church were shut.

Then he saw him.

Ian Richardson, sauntering up to the church rather nonchalantly. Bareheaded. Casually dressed, as always.

Richardson now did the same as Golly. He looked at his watch. Then he went over to the two phone booths and stood. Waiting.

He wasn't expecting to see anyone. But he was probably anticipating that tonight Golly would use the system and phone the number.

To report that John Chance was dead.

Richardson stood, waiting.

76

Golly came up from behind.

"Good evening, Ian," he said.

Richardson swung around.

"You bloody fool," he said. His eyes lurched all over the street, quickly. Then back to Golly, angrily.

"Get away, quickly," said Richardson. "Don't talk. Just move away."

"Nobody's around," said Golly quietly. He nearly said, nobody knows, but that would have been a lie.

"It isn't safe," hissed Richardson. "Not like this."

Suddenly his eyes narrowed.

"How did you know I was using this phone booth tonight?" he almost whispered.

"Come along, Ian," said Golly lightly. "The 229 exchange is Bayswater. The rest isn't too difficult . . ."

"Call me tomorrow," said Richardson, and swung around on his heel. He started walking off.

"Ian," said Golly, softly.

He stopped, turned slowly. "Did you get him?" he asked.

Golly shook his head.

"Get on with it, then. And stop playing stupid games."

He looked furious. Golly came up to him. There was nobody around. A car honked somewhere, but it wasn't near them.

"I'm sorry, Ian," said Golly. He had the gun in his hand, and it was pointing at Richardson.

The haughty eyes that could see both ways opened like a curtain that was lifted slightly.

"Of course," the man called Ian Richardson said, almost to himself.

His high cheekbones flushed.

Golly fired twice. It hardly made a sound. Just two thuds.

Richardson straightened up, as if he had been struck a blow.

"Mikhail," he said. "Mikhail, you got the wrong man . . . Take care . . ."

Then he fell headlong and lay still.

A small pool of blood began to form under him.

Golly looked around. Nobody. Nothing.

He walked across the road quickly, then into the side turning. His heart was pounding. But he also knew he had got away with it.

He clutched the pistol in his jacket pocket. It hadn't even kicked when he fired. It was a smooth weapon, beautifully tooled. It made it all so easy. Just a squeeze and . . .

In the Bayswater Road, Golly stopped. There were people about. Strolling, laughing, a couple with their arms around each other, three black men debating earnestly as they carried their dirty laundry in plastic bags.

And only a few hundred yards away, around the corner, sprawled in front of a phone kiosk, lay the body of the man he had just killed.

And suddenly Golly felt sick.

Because Richardson had said the wrong thing.

No hate. No curses. No threats.

Instead, his last words were "Take care."

Concern. For the man who was killing him.

It was all wrong. Richardson should have said things like, Don't be a fool, we'll get you. You can't get away with this . . . we know who you are anyway.

But all he did was to care for Golly at the end.

Like a dying soldier on the battlefield, killed by a terrible mistake, trying to warn his comrade with his last breath.

"Take care."

Golly walked on, blindly, unseeing.

He had killed the wrong man.

Yet the right man had given the order.

Viktor Fedorovitch was Central. No imposter, no impersonator, no substitute. The real thing.

But Richardson was the wrong man.

Which meant that John Chance . . .

Yet it was Chance who had proved himself, who was working with the major.

It was like being trapped in a maze, in which every turning leads to a new path that only brings one back to the start.

A maze that has no exit, except . . .

Yes. That was it.

Golly made up his mind.

It was his last-ever chance. In just over an hour John

Chance would pick them up. They'd be in their hands forever.

They must vanish, he and Sharon. The passports were ready in the drawer. So were the blank tickets to Rome. He hadn't booked a flight, but there still might be one that evening. If not, they could fly to Paris and go on to Rome in the morning. Anywhere.

The important thing was to disappear. Now. In the next hour. Before John Chance turned up.

Golly jumped into a cab. It was only two or three minutes to the flat, but every minute was precious.

Precious. You could say that again. Life or death.

Because, for him, the ghost existence was at an end.

The illegal life could be no more. He wasn't being disloyal. He wasn't going to betray anyone. He wasn't changing sides.

He was getting out.

He wasn't going to work for them—or *them*.

Not ever again.

He didn't want to know who was bluffing whom, which joker was trumping which ace.

He just wanted to live with Sharon. Unknown, unwanted, unimportant.

The cab drew up outside the house. Golly paid and rushed in.

77

"Sharon!" he called out, as soon as he'd let himself into the flat. "Where are you?"

She came into the hall. She looked very pretty.

"Do you like it?" she said. "I got the sweater in Bond Street today."

"It's lovely," he said automatically. Then:

"Look, I haven't got time to explain. You've got to throw a few things in a case. We're off in ten minutes."

She stood rock still.

"Off to where?"

How do you explain it? How do you say, I am about to be no more?

"We've got to get out of the country," he said.

"What, now?"

She looked baffled.

"Straightaway. Hurry up."

Her mind seemed to be elsewhere.

"All my things are at the cleaners," she said, as if that were the one reason why they couldn't go.

He grabbed her hand, dragged her into the living room, and sat her down.

"I can't explain. Not now," he said.

"Oh, Mike. What's happened?"

Her beautiful eyes looked so sad.

He wanted to say, I've killed a man. I may have killed the wrong man. I don't know. I don't know any more which side I am on. I don't know if I am a traitor or a hero. I know nothing except that we must get out of it.

"What's wrong?" she said, full of concern.

He stood up.

"I'll tell you on the way to the airport. For God's sake, get going."

"The airport." She stood up. "Where are we . . ."

"I don't know. Paris. Rome. Brussels. Anywhere. Out of England . . ."

"I've got to call Mother," she said.

"There isn't time," he yelled at her. He looked at his watch. John Chance would be there in forty minutes.

"We can't go like this," said Sharon. "It's insane. When will we be back?"

And what could he say? Never, maybe?

"I don't know yet," he said.

"Mike, this is crazy."

She said it very calmly.

He tried to collect himself.

"Look, you have to believe me," he said, trying to sound perfectly rational. "This is our only chance."

"*Our* only chance?"

220

"To start a new life. You and me. A real life. To escape."

She frowned. "Escape what? You don't make sense."

He pushed her toward the door.

"For pity's sake, love, grab your things. We've got to get out."

She stared at him puzzled. But she left the room. She let herself be navigated into the hall.

In the living room, Golly sat in the armchair, mentally checking his list. Passports. Yes. Tickets yes. The traveler's checks were in the drawer, thank God.

His shirt was soaked. He felt feverish. In his mind's eye, he saw Ian Richardson. The blood.

"Take care."

His last words. His last thoughts. For somebody else. For his killer.

He went over and helped himself to a drink. He was shaking. He needed it badly. In a couple of hours, everything would be all right. They'd be away. He had to be calm.

It was just after seven. God, Chance would be here in twenty-five minutes. They had to get out. He went to the door.

"Sharon," he called out. He started to say "Hurry up . . ."

But he never finished.

Sharon was standing there already.

"You're not going anywhere, Mikhail," she said.

All Golly saw was the gun in her hand.

78

He thought he was going mad. "What the hell's that?" he gasped. Sharon's hand was very steady. He could see the finger curled around the trigger. She looked determined.

"Sit down again," said Sharon. It was an order. Golly backed into the living room but he kept staring at the gun. It pointed at him, unwavering.

"Over there," she said, indicating the armchair. She perched herself on a corner of the table, swinging one leg casually.

And the gun kept pointing at him.

"Sharon," he said. His voice croaked. "What are you doing with that thing?"

"Just sit and don't move."

"I don't understand," he faltered.

His numbed mind began to realize the full implication of what she had called him. Mikhail.

"It's very simple. You're staying here. In fact, we both are."

Golly closed his eyes for a second, like someone who hopes that if he can shut out the nightmare, it will go away. But when he opened them, she was still there, with the gun. Looking at him a little sadly.

"I never wanted it this way. Believe me," she said, "but there's no choice."

"What's this all about?" he asked. Golly felt like a drowning man in a sea of questions.

"It's all over, Mikhail," she said matter-of-factly. "You're finished. You've done what we wanted. Your usefulness is at an end. We don't need you any more."

"We? Who the devil are you talking about? I don't even understand you. Who's *we*?"

Sharon sighed a little wearily. "Who do you think? John Chance. My people. It's taken us years and it's all worked out perfectly."

"You and John Chance," he said.

"Yes, Mikhail. From the moment you came to this country, we've been watching you and following you and listening to you. You have never been alone. We've always been there waiting for the moment to use you and then destroy you." Sharon seemed amazingly impersonal. As if she were discussing some abstract concept.

"You!" he gasped. All the time. Together, close to each other, sharing the intimacies of days and nights, being one. And all the time . . .

"Is that all you cared about?" he asked.

Momentarily her hand with the gun wavered slightly.

"Does it matter?" she said. "Now?"

He nodded.

"We've been doing the same thing, that's all," she said. "We're sleepers. We've been sleeping together for three years. In every sense, but for different people."

He felt drained suddenly. "That's all it's been to you? Orders? All our time together? Just a job?"

Her eyes flashed.

"Haven't you been pretending, lying, cheating. Using me? What have you been doing over the past seven years but living a lie? And you've been quite happy to make me part of that lie."

"I loved you," he said.

"Because it helped your cover," she said bitterly. "Because it was convenient. Don't pretend with me, Mikhail. Even the name was a lie."

"I had no choice," he said dully.

"No?" she challenged and laughed without humor.

Golly swallowed. "They've got my daughter over there. She's being well looked after. As long as . . ."

"I know," she said.

He suddenly felt angry. "Spare me the sermon," he snapped. "*You* have a choice. You don't have to do this. Nobody has a hold over you."

"You're right," she said and she almost tossed her head defiantly. "I didn't have to do anything. Nobody made me. I wanted to. I chose to." Sharon was almost proud.

He had never seen a Sharon like this. He thought he knew her in all her moods. Soft, feminine, fun. Vulnerable and insecure. But this was a different woman. A stranger whom he had never kissed, with whom he had never slept. This was an enemy.

He stared at her, baffled. "So why are you doing this to me?"

She shook her head.

"It doesn't really matter why," she said. "It's not you. It's what you do. The reason you are here. The people you work for. I am paying them back, just a little . . ."

"I don't understand," said Golly. "Why? How?"

"I made sure I would get recruited," she went on, as if he hadn't spoken. "The British are very good for talent scouting, aren't they? At places like universities, the BBC, Fleet Street, language schools. The right place at the right time. I got the right kind of job. I knew they'd find me, with my background. And they did."

Sharon studied him.

"The service was quite surprised how much I could hate. That I was prepared to do anything. *Anything.* So they found me a very special assignment. You. You needed my kind of dedication. And I gave it, didn't I?"

He realized for the first time how dangerous she was. Only now it was too late.

"But why do you hate so?" he asked, very quietly.

Sharon sighed. "If I told you that my father had his legs blown off by one of your mines when he tried to flee over the Wall. That he lay for three hours on the death strip, screaming, bleeding to death, that every time somebody tried to reach him from the other side your people opened fire to keep them away, that they watched him die very slowly. . . He couldn't even scream any more . . ."

"I never knew," said Golly.

"No. You thought I was a nice, well-brought-up English girl from a dull suburban family. I'm English, all right, Mikhail, and I do go to the suburbs to visit my mother and my sister, but my father came from a different world. Your world. And you killed him."

She shrugged. "They needed somebody for this kind of work. They need girls who do what I'm doing to you. So I volunteered. I had good reason, hadn't I?"

"And you and I? It was just an assignment?"

"Correct, Mikhail. They told me to pick up this enemy sleeper, to make myself available to him, to infiltrate him."

Golly winced.

224

"That's right. Make him want you in bed. Get him to trust you, to rely on you, to believe in you, and help us trap him."

He stood up.

"I'm going," he said.

She straightened herself off the table, the gun aimed at him. "Don't," she warned.

"You going to kill me, Sharon?" He smiled. "You want me to believe that? Just like that? After all that's . . ."

"I mean it," she said.

"Your friends are coming for me and I'm not going to be here," he said. "They won't find me."

"You've only got one chance," she said coldly. "To use that gun in your pocket. To kill me before I kill you."

Golly turned to the door. "Good-bye," he said.

"Don't make me do it," she whispered.

"Good-bye," he repeated and stepped into the doorway.

He really believed she would not fire. But when the shot came it smashed into the framed picture, shattering the glass. The bullet had passed over his shoulder.

He turned slowly. She was standing there, tense.

"I have five more bullets," she said.

"Let me go," he said quietly.

"If I have to, I'll kill you," she said, and there was a tear in her eye.

"No . . ." She could never . . . "You wouldn't."

"There are two of me, Mike," she said. "There's the one you know. And there's this one. This one isn't very nice."

"I only know the girl I met at that party three years ago. The girl I fell in love with . . ."

"Who was acting on orders the whole time," she said. "And I'm not going to break them now. Sorry, Mike."

The doorbell rang.

"You'd better go and answer it," she said.

He shook his head.

"Please," she said, and the gun was on him.

He shuffled to the door, Sharon walking behind him, the gun never leaving his back.

The bell rang again.

"Open it," she said.

In the door stood John Chance. Behind him was a man who seemed vaguely familiar.

"Hello, Mike," said John Chance. "May we come in?"

They entered the hall, and Chance saw the gun in Sharon's hand.

"Are you all right?" he asked.

She nodded.

"Any trouble?"

"No," she said. "No trouble at all."

Chance gave her a sharp look. Then he turned to Golly.

"Sorry, Mike, it's all over for you," he said.

Golly's eyes were still on Sharon. Chance took it in. The white, stricken face, the desperate look.

"Your people would do the same to us," he said. "It's a rough trade. And it hasn't been easy for her, either."

The other man stepped forward.

"Michael Golly, alias Mikhail Pyotr Bauer, alias Mike Walker, alias Michael Geiler."

"Yes," said Golly, still looking at Sharon.

"I am Detective Chief Inspector Woodham of Special Branch, and I am arresting you for the murder of Ian Richardson, alias Nicolai Stepanovich Sergoff, about an hour ago."

"I understand," said Golly.

Golly nodded again. He knew where he had seen that man. He had worn dungarees in the tall office building in Tottenham Court Road.

He looked at John Chance.

"Who are you?" he said. He seemed to have aged.

"Mike, you know me," said Chance. "You know my name. It is my name."

"Who are you?" repeated Golly. He was almost begging.

"Who I said I was when we first met. Ministry of Defence."

"And she?"

Sharon had lowered her gun. She stood silent.

"The same."

"Planted on me, at that party years ago."

"I don't think you had such a bad bargain," said John Chance, a little hard.

"Shall we go?" said Michael Golly, looking at John Chance.

"I'll have your gun," said Woodham, taking it out of Golly's pocket. He had some handcuffs.

"Hold out your hands," he said gruffly.

"I don't think that's necessary," said John Chance. "I don't think he's got anywhere to go."

79

"I don't like the way this man operates," sniffed Sir Deryck.

"John Chance has achieved everything he set out to do," said Foxglove.

"He. Always he. What *he* set out to do. We are a team. We should work as a team. These solo efforts . . ."

"A few of us helped," said Foxglove.

"It was his operation. He set out to destroy their section. He was responsible for the, ahem, accident to that man Hentoff."

"Possibly," said Foxglove cautiously.

"You know he was," snapped Sir Deryck. "He killed the sleeper's control. He woke up the sleeper and used him as bait to bring Sergoff over. Then he used the sleeper to kill Sergoff. Very nasty."

"Very successful."

"They'll retaliate," said Sir Deryck. "I warn you,

they won't take this lying down. They'll do it to us. Something just as nasty."

"We'll just have to wait and see, won't we?"

"Hmm," said Sir Deryck. If he phrased the report to the Prime Minister the right way, he could get a good deal of kudos.

"This defector, what's happened to him?"

"He's singing to the CIA like Tito Gobbi."

"We've no longer got him?"

"He did his bit. He convinced Mr. Golly. That's all we wanted from him."

"Ah, yes. Mr. Golly. What about him?"

"He will get life," said Foxglove, brushing an invisible thread off his knee. "That is the only sentence a judge can pass for murder."

"Nasty," said Sir Deryck. "He was used."

"Naturally," said Foxglove. "What else was he there for?"

80

In New York, Kahn sat between two gray-suited men in the back of a black car.

"I don't know what you guys want with me," growled Kahn.

"I think you do," said the older of the two. Both were federal agents.

"I want a lawyer," said Kahn.

"You know your rights," said the older agent.

"What's it all about anyway?" said Kahn. "You bust into my deli, you grab me, I get hustled into this heap— What the hell is going on?"

"Espionage," said the agent. "That's what's going on."

"I don't know what you're talking about," said Kahn.

"Three Two to Three One," crackled the radio.

"Three One," said the third federal agent, who was

sitting in front, beside the driver. They also both wore gray suits.

"Three Two to Three One," said the radio. "Madison okay. Repeat, Madison okay."

"Three One roger," said the man with the radio-telephone.

The older agent said to Kahn:

"That's another one of your friends taken care of."

Kahn looked stonily ahead, at the heads in front of him.

They were near the East River when the radio came on the air again.

"Three Four to Three One," it murmured.

The man beside the driver acknowledged.

"Three Four to Three One, Lexington okay."

The older agent nudged Kahn.

"That's the lady who likes to play chess. You're all in the bag, the whole damn shoot. All inside."

Kahn turned his head, and he looked straight at the older agent, and he smiled.

"Are we?" he said. "Are we, really?"

He was still smiling when they led him, hands manacled, into the FBI building.

81

In an apartment in Queens, the sandy-haired man read of the arrests that night and sighed. He would have to start from scratch.

82

The colonel knew what it was all about when he entered his office on the third floor and saw the burly figure standing behind his desk, looking out of the window.

"Hello, Sakharof," said the colonel.

The burly figure turned around, its granite features cracking into a false smile.

"My dear Alexander, I was just admiring the view," he said.

"Yes," said the colonel.

Sakharof cleared his throat.

"I hope you didn't mind my making myself at home," he said politely.

"Why not?" replied the colonel. "This is your home now."

"How nice to be made welcome," said Sakharof. "Before you take your well-deserved leave, perhaps we can spend a couple of days going through things."

"Yes," said the colonel.

"To bring me up to date," said Sakharof. "On everything."

Everything. Viktor Fedorovitch defecting. Hentoff dead. Sergoff dead. Golly arrested. London smashed. New York almost destroyed. All at the betrayal of Viktor Fedorovitch. The man who sold out years ago, double-faced from the start.

"Do not worry if things are a little bit in chaos," purred Sakharof. "You have had your problems lately, I know."

"We have lost a lot of good people," said the colonel. "The work of years."

"Don't fret about it. It was a pity you never suspected him," said Sakharof. "I will pick up the pieces and put everything together again."

He beamed at the colonel.

"Have you had your new assignment yet?"

The son of a pig. He'd really like to dance on my grave, thought the colonel.

But aloud he said only, "Yes."

"May one ask where?"

Sakharof was playing coy, but he intended to make the colonel say it.

"Kiev." He bit it out.

"Alexander, you are so lucky," said Sakharof with a

230

show of delight. "What a beautiful city. And the post?"

All right. Make me crawl.

"Railway police."

"Ah, yes." Even Sakharof came to a halt. From this key command to a railway police office in the provinces. They might as well have sent him to Manchuria. He was finished.

"Well," said Sakharof at last, "I'm sure you'll find it very restful. I'll send you some English cigarettes."

"I have some things to do," said the colonel. "Perhaps if we meet tomorrow . . ."

"You are departing that soon?"

"Within twenty-four hours."

He was only echoing the general.

"Very good, Alexander," said Sakharof. "Tomorrow then. Here. At nine."

Half an hour later, an aide laid a Tass message from London on the colonel's desk.

It reported, briefly, that Michael Golly, a manufacturer, had pleaded guilty at the Old Bailey to a charge of murder and had been jailed for life. As it was a guilty plea, no evidence had been called and the trial lasted only nine minutes.

The British were playing it by the rules. They didn't mind soiling the laundry, but it would never be washed in public.

83

There was one visitor for Golly.

"Hello, Mike," she said.